AF777628

The Soul of Poland

Ina Steinberg

Llumina Press

© 2013 Ina Steinberg

All rights reserved. No part of this publication may be reproduced or transmitted in any form or by any means electronic or mechanical, including photocopy, recording, or any information storage and retrieval system, without permission in writing from both the copyright owner and the publisher.

Requests for permission to make copies of any part of this work should be mailed to Permissions Department, Llumina Press, 7101 W. Commercial Blvd., Ste. 4E, Tamarac, FL 33319

ISBN: 978-1-60594-994-9 (PB)

Printed in the United States of America by Llumina Press

Library of Congress Control Number: 2012920744

Acknowledgements

Many thanks to my friends and colleagues who provided material and data as well as support for the writing of this novel. My gratitude goes to Tadeusz Babij. Ph.D., Professor Emeritus, Florida International University, for providing me with helpful materials and wonderful conversations about Poland during the period covered.

I also wish to express my appreciation to Monika Knapp and her skilled and efficient staff at the Helen B. Hoffman Plantation Library. Their strong desire to help does make research in their holdings very enjoyable and productive.

My thanks also to Elizabeth Will, for her excellent comments and support and to Christine Newman, a member of the Friends of the Library group in Plantation, for the excellent materials about Poland which she made available to me. And, of course, at the base of everything, rests my thanks to Pete, who always makes all things possible for me.

Chapter 1

"But why?" asked Paul, his eyes sweeping Mariana's face as if he would find his answer there.

Under most circumstances there are few moments more agreeable or productive each day than those spent with friends, especially when that person is Princess Mariana Novikova, Paul Duke's most level headed and devoted friend. However, Paul's present moments with Mariana were far from agreeable.

There sat Paul, head in hand next to her in the comfortable kitchen, doing what the two of them jokingly called their "weekly household bill paying session," a session which usually became a fun chat or a gourmet cooking session rather than any dry weekly disbursements of money.

However, the look on Paul's face said very clearly that today there would be no chatting.

He cut right to the core. "Why haven't they called me, Mariana?" he asked. "It's 1939 and everyone knows that the impending Nazi invasion of Poland is getting closer and closer. Everyone, even an idiot, knows that this means war."

The "they" Paul referred to was the SIS, the Secret Intelligence Service of British Intelligence that Paul worked for.

In other words, Paul was a British spy.

Looking at his unhappy face, Mariana felt a wave of love for him. He had become such a part of their family that she never attempted to understand why she felt as she did about him. It just seemed right to have him with them to share a life that he helped make satisfying.

Waiting for the sauce to boil she thought about what the reasons might be for his depression.

"The SIS will call you when the moment is right," she said to soothe him. "Don't you remember, dear, that those were the exact words of the SIS director in London when he told you two years ago to relocate our family to Switzerland?" Paul had lived with the Novikovs so long that he and they considered him family.

Paul shook his head. "That doesn't mean a thing. It must be that the SIS doesn't want me."

For a second she hesitated as if his words were disturbing her vision of reality. A sudden rush throbbed in her head when she thought about how diminished life would be without him. She recovered when she viewed the familiar objects of their kitchen--the black, aged Aga, the table and chairs pockmarked with both scratches as well as memories of laughing times spent together, the work table where biscuits were always rising—and the wonderful smells of cinnamon and other spices that always delighted one's nose on entering the room. For a moment she wondered about the source of any happiness, whether it be specifically the happiness which a friendship such as Paul's brings or whether it be the smells of a well-used kitchen. It must be tied to one's comfort level, she decided, for above all else, her relationship with Paul was comforting. He might be a private person, to be sure. Probably he was, as she would guess, one of those fortunate few who would rather be content with their own company than be forced to tolerate the tiresome and banal. However, Mariana was well aware that when he loved, he loved deeply.

"Could the birthday you celebrated last month be the cause of your depression, rather than the SIS?"

"Of course not," he answered much too quickly.

Mariana shifted gears. That approach hadn't worked. How about another? "Then look at the positives of your career."

He merely sniffed at that, although Mariana sensed an opening.

"Let me remind you that you are the only intelligence agent in British history ever presented with a knighthood. That came from a very grateful King George V in 1920. And also let me remind you of how many Russian lives you saved when the Russian Revolution began. We Novikovs are living proof of how expertly you smuggled people out of Russia."

"That was my job."

"And you've always been successful at it." She continued relentlessly. "The SIS has always used you to mentor new agents. Would they do that if you weren't top flight?"

"Certainly." A moment of silence and then some blustery words from him to the effect that he had a mind to sit down and write out his letter of resignation before he received one of termination.

Mariana was not as alarmed by his threats as he supposed she would be. He was disappointed. Couldn't she understand how hurt he was? He waited expectantly for her support.

Of course she did know how hurt he was. But privately, Mariana alone knew how many versions of Paul there were to counter the Paul who hurt. There was Paul the expert spy, for one; Paul the cunning adventurer, for another; Paul the academician whose knowledge of history was formidable; Paul the fighter for basic human rights, Paul the lover of music, and yes, even Paul the romantic figure whose pain from his unrequited love for Alexa only she knew about.

Oh, yes, Paul was a special person who was loved by the entire Novikov family.

However, Mariana touched none of these in her response to the Paul who stood in front of her.

"Get over it. Do straighten up and be more patient," was how she counseled Paul the Irate.

After that, she folded her arms and stared at him with the conviction of a woman who refuses to be awed by such a piddling and inconsequential vice as disappointment.

Paul could not have been more startled if Winston Churchill himself had just walked into the Novikov kitchen and summoned him back to duty.

"I do have to be more patient, I suppose," he acknowledged.

"Of course, my dear. Stop underestimating yourself. You have saved lives. I know that I trust you with my life." Indeed, Mariana had done just that years ago.

"Just as I trust you, Mariana."

A friend to Andrei Novikov from their student days at Oxford, Paul had literally led the three Novikovs from St. Petersburg to the safety of Paris when the Russian Revolution began. Once the wealthiest family in Russia, the Novikovs had lost everything they owned except for what Paul managed to bring out of Russia for them, Since then the SIS subsidized all the expenses of the Novikovs, allowing them to live comfortably first in France and now Switzerland. When World War II began to loom, the SIS concluded that because of Swiss neutrality the Novikov home in Zurich would make an ideal base for Paul to collect information about the Nazis.

The telephone on the kitchen table began to jangle.

Mariana laughed. "You see, Paul? I bet that Churchill is calling you."

Paul smiled. "More than not it is the butcher calling for our weekly meat order," he said. However, his body stiffened after he picked up the phone and listened for a few seconds.

"Yes, sir," he said to the voice on the other end.

Looking at Mariana he pointed to the receiver and whispered, "It i*s* Churchill."

"Stop your tricks, Paul. I'm not falling for that," she hissed.

Paul returned to the caller. "Of course I will be there. Thank you." Paul hung up. "It *was* Churchill."

There was awe in his voice. "I have to leave for London tonight." Gone was his depression. And reinvigorated was his sense of duty. He had been told by Churchill to meet in England as soon as possible with Hugh Dalton, certainly one of Paul's least favorite English intelligence officers, but a higher-ranked officer than Paul was, nonetheless.

"Did I hear the word leave?" Alexa Novikova said on entering the kitchen.

Alexa was beautiful. There was no doubt about that. Her wheat-colored blonde hair hung in silken rivulets of curls that would never stay behind her ears. Her face had a fragile, vulnerable loveliness to it, much like a portrait of an 18th century princess removed from the coarse necessities of the world. She was dressed in a black cashmere sweater with a silk scarf at the throat and beige cashmere slacks that accentuated her lovely figure.

There had never been a time during all the years Paul had known Alexa, his friend Andrei's wife, when her presence had not affected him. He might be ashamed of it, but he had never found a way to control the pounding his heart made when she entered a room. It made him want to scream, to plead, to implore. He thought her beautiful, but he saw hers as a beauty linked to intelligence and compassion. It was that linkage which gave him such pleasure to be in her presence. More than anything else, it was a love that made him immeasurably sad because it forced him to realize that nothing he could say would ever reach her. Oh, yes. He knew the pain of love very well. *Come away with me,my dear,* was what he wanted to say. *I love you, Alexa. I always have. That selfish idiot of a husband of yours can't make you happy. He never will. But I can. Give me a chance. Please.*

But he wondered if he had a right to wish for such a thing. After all, could he ever make anyone happy? Hadn't Helena found that out a year into their marriage? He had come home one day to find the results of not making her happy. Hadn't she walked out after a year of marriage? All she left was a note on the table: *It isn't working. I will get a divorce. Helena.*

No "I'm sorry," no "let's talk," ever came from her. It was as if Helena thought him a cipher. And perhaps he was. No one knew about that early marriage of his, not even the Novikovs. Nor would anyone ever learn about it from him. The phrase *It isn't working. . .it isn't working. .* .often hammered in his head, particularly during those long black nights when sleep won't come.

He had learned to be quite adept at hiding his emotions through the years. He called it his self-sufficiency factor. It comforted him to know that no one else ever saw his grief. Only Mariana sensed something, feeling his sadness, and knowing full well what caused it. It was her fear, however, that the more Paul attempted to control his emotions the more he might narrow his options for what he expected from life. She did not want that to happen.

Mariana also believed that Alexa and Paul could make each other happy if Alexa were ever strong enough to make the break from Andrei. As for her son Andrei, Mariana knew that he was hopeless—lovable, charming, and happy—but hopeless, nonetheless. It distressed both Paul and Mariana to realize that Alexa was little more than a valued possession of Andrei's, someone who made him content only because she had agreed to the other lovers in his life. Had Andrei ever uncovered Paul's feelings for Alexa, Mariana assumed that he probably would have felt pleased rather than angry. The more others admired Andrei's possessions, the more it affirmed to him that one of his most prized attributes was his innate good sense.

"What happened?" Alexa asked, noting the looks on the faces of Paul and Mariana.

"I must leave for London tonight," Paul explained. "But I will be back in a few days, hopefully. There is a plane waiting at the Zurich airport right now to fly me to London to meet with the SIS."

Alexa looked relieved to hear that the SIS had promised that he would return to Switzerland. She had known of Paul's desire to get back into intelligence work.

"Are those bills that I see in your hand, Alexa?" Mariana reached out for them.

Alexa nodded. "I was bringing them to you and Paul. More of Andrei's clothing bills."

"And where is that tailor's best friend at this moment?" Mariana asked, realizing that she hadn't seen her son Andrei for a while.

"He and his friend Andrew are at the Munich Music Festival for a few days,"Alexa said brightly.

"And so you are here alone while he is away with his new friend of the week? Wasn't it a house party in Lausanne with Dan last weekend and Biarritz with Reginald the weekend before that?" Mariana's voice was tight.

"Don't be angry at him," pleaded Alexa. "Andrei's energy level is high. He constantly needs people and new activities to keep him happy, He had everything taken away from him by the Russian Revolution. It's always easier to live with loss if you've never tasted the delicacy of possession."

Paul and Mariana had heard that drivel of an excuse from Alexa before. Privately, Paul wondered if Andrei hadn't tasted more than his share of the "delicacies" that Alexa mentioned. She treated Andrei as some kind of god, Paul thought angrily. Paul had no intention of ever doing that.

Nor did Mariana. "We all lost our previous lives when the Revolution came," she reminded Alexa. "You talk about

Andrei's happiness, but what about yours? Wouldn't you appreciate a loyal and faithful husband instead of what you have?" She had the word "philanderer" on the tip of her tongue, but caught herself in time.

Alexa ignored the questions. "Please understand." Her voice had acquired the panicky quality it always got when her relationship with Andrei was threatened. Usually a soft low voice, her voice had a tendency to rise slightly in pitch when she was upset. Paul called it the "curse of the Romanovs." He knew of no one in the dynasty who didn't have the tendency to slightly squeak when upset.

Mariana pressed. "But what about that life of yours? Is your life anything more than a huge waiting room in which my son throws you a kiss every now and then before he goes off on another escapade?" She paused. "Leave him, child."

"Never. He needs me." That was the excuse Alexa always gave when she felt cornered.

"He's my son. But his actions to you are often cruel."

The room was quiet so that all they could hear were the soft sounds of Alexa's pain. Paul shook his head at Mariana. All Mariana was achieving was upsetting Alexa. Paul was certain that Alexa was in love with what Andrei represented, not the man himself. However, only by examining her own heart would Alex ever learn the difference between the idea and the reality of love. Paul seriously doubted if she was capable of such self scrutiny.

But he could certainly understand why Alexa was awed by her husband. Andrei was bigger than life. And it wasn't just arrogance on Andrei's part. His perspective stemmed from having once led a life that gave him everything he desired without question. In the world that Andrei had once inhabited one could seek entrance only if Andrei had first approved the request. In spite of the fact that such a world was gone, it seemed as if both Andrei and Alexa would never accept its disappearance.

Paul shook his head when Mariana continued to berate Andrei to Alexa. It wouldn't help.

Alexa's tears reminded him of the awful story that Mariana had lived through years ago. Although he hadn't been there, Paul would never forget what he'd learned from Mariana about the early days of the marriage of Andrei and Alexa.

Theirs had been a spectacular marriage ceremony, the kind that can only occur when the richest man in Russia—including even the tsar and his holdings—marries the beautiful niece of the tsar.

However, according to Mariana, Alexa had confronted Andrei only three weeks into their marriage to ask him to stop his affairs with his lovers and to end his unexpected weekend trips.

"Or?" he asked quietly. Before giving her time to respond he turned and walked out of the room and down the hall steps. She caught up with him at the front door, reaching out to hold him and keep him from leaving.

"I won't complain again," she cried. "I promise."

After Alexa cut her wrists later that day in an attempt at suicide, Andrei was advised by her doctor to explain to her the limits of the marriage he expected them to have. After Andrei told her what that involved, Alexa closed her eyes and raised his hand to her lips.

"Can't you love me?" she asked.

Not in the way she wanted, he told her. And he had no desire to be in love, he said.

Mariana approached Andrei two days later to tell him that Alexa would accept his terms. She would accept him for what he was willing to give. In return, he would keep his private life from her.

Paul often thought about the contract Andrei and Alexa had made those many years ago. By agreeing to it hadn't

Alexa made herself a victim as well as her own executioner? But Paul had to stop thinking about Alexa. He looked at his watch and realized that he needed to hurry in order to make his plane.

He said, "Before I go, there are some things I want to say to the two of you. First, let's keep the fact that Churchill called today between the three of us. Right?" They understood. Andrei had a reputation for having a loose mouth.

"There is something else. Sometime I want to discuss at length more about what Mariana and I have said to you today, Alexa. But not not now. When times are better and we're not distracted by the war that's coming, then we'll talk." He looked at her and said, "All we want is for you to be happy." But what he wanted was larger than that. He wanted to take Alexa into his arms and never let her go.

Alexa took his hand. "We'll talk later. Just come back to us."

They shoved all of the bills that they had been working on into a kitchen drawer for later so that the two women might help Paul pack.

"I'll ride with you to the airport," Mariana said when their chauffeur started putting Paul's luggage into the car trunk.

"I can't stand watching any more of Alexa's unhappiness," said Paul when the car carrying Mariana and him pulled away.

"I know," she said. "Perhaps a distraction for a while is what you need."

"Putting it on a back burner is all I can manage," he confessed. "You were right about the effect of my birthday. We're getting old, you and I," Paul said.

"But we both wear well. Although you are looking exceptionally tired today, I must say."

"I feel tired."

Mariana looked at him in alarm. She reached out and took his arm.

"Paul, please don't change. You've always been the one we lean on. I'm selfish enough to want that Paul to be with us always."

She was asking him not to change, not to alter himself. He felt a frustrating helplessness at the request. He wondered if it were caused by time. He was changing; he felt it inside him. Whether his new assignment at SIS succeeded or failed, he wondered whether he wanted to continue to be the same man. Would time outwit him? From now on he would try to consider every moment of happiness as a separate success. He was also surprised to discover that he was beginning to doubt his own power to succeed. After all, what did he have to show for the last few years of his life? He knew with a dreadful clarity that he wanted his life to be different. He wanted a fuller, different life. He also had a sobering thought. Suppose Alexa was more in love with suffering than with anything or anyone? How could he deal with that? If that were true, there was no hope for him. None at all.

A half hour later they approached the airport.

"I'm sorry, Mariana," he said, attempting to rouse himself from his own dreary thoughts. "It must be oxygen deprivation. Can you open the window on your side? That's better. And can you give me some food from the hamper which you and Alexa put together for me for the flight? I'll be fine," he assured her. "Check on me twenty years from now and you'll probably find me facing the same problems. The only difference is that I'll be older. But I won't have changed. I guarantee it." However, giving such a guarantee to her only added to his depression.

They had reached the airport.

"Goodbye, darling," Mariana said as she hugged him. "Come back to us as soon as possible."

♦

Little was Paul aware that in another part of what was soon to be a war-torn world, circumstances were being put in motion that might make his return to Switzerland an uncertain thing.

"Try to be quiet, " whispered one of the three men. It was late at night and everyone and every noise in the small Polish village outside Krakow would be seen or heard.

"Shoes reverberate on the wooden floors unless you tread softly," he added.

The two other men obediently followed him and walked silently into the cabin.

"These bags are filled with materials about science. That means books, magazines, notes—anything that we could find. Scatter it around the cabin so that it looks as if a scientist lived here," said the first man.

They worked quietly but quickly. Soon fifteen bags of materials had been scattered around the cabin. "A scientist certainly lived here, but a very sloppy scientist," added one of the men.

"Don't forget to remind de Wiart to send a copy of the death notice to the local newspapers in Krakow," said one man, as he looked around the house approvingly. "I've already sent a letter to the man who will pose as the dead man's cousin. And our Berlin contact was also sent the details. Anyone would believe that important scientific work was done in this cabin."

"Good. Now let's get out of here."

Chapter 2

Friedrich-Werner Graf von der Schulenburg was an authentic German aristocrat.

There was no doubt about that.

From the "Graf " in his name---German for "count,"-- to his straight-as-a-poker spine, to the way he marched, not walked—Friedrich-Werner Graf von der Schulenburg was a German aristocrat. His home, *Burg Fulkenberg,* a castle in the Upper Palatinate replete with wife and children, was eminently appropriate for one with the aristocratic cache which one of his station possessed. A pride in Germany and the noble history which his ancestors had helped to accumulate had also motivated his lifelong desire to achieve the dizzying amount of public service he did amass in his sixty-two years. This service included four stints in the military as well as a diplomatic career which began before World War I in Barcelona and continued in such locations as Prague, Warsaw, Bucharest, Teheran, Russia, and a short stay in Tbilisi.

Indeed, by 1939 Friedrich-Werner Graf von der Schulenburg was a passionately loyal German aristocrat. However, he was also a passionately loyal German aristocrat who could hate just as passionately as he could love.

And who was the current object of that virulent hatred?

Adolph Hitler.

In that respect, Friedrich was far from alone. Like many of his military aristocratic colleagues, he considered Hitler and members of the Nazi party as little more than nameless, low-class vermin, or at best, certainly no more than temporary aberrations on the proud face of Germany. He had grown frustrated with the world. Why couldn't everyone see that Hitler would back down if everyone stood up to him? Friedrich's friends had no answer to that question, or even more importantly, most of them lacked the courage to stand up to anyone, let alone Hitler. In ticking off the names of high German military leaders Friedrich could name only a few with the guts to follow through and rid Germany of Hitler.

One was Admiral Wilhelm Franz Canaris, leader of the *Abwer*, the clandestine and powerful Nazi German intelligence service located in Berlin.

However, even with the popular Canaris it was problematical as to whether he would get any support from Germans if he acted against Hitler. The truth was that, aside from Canaris and a few others, Germany's military leaders tended to talk a good game, but not to act. Meanwhile, Hitler continued to intimidate the world with a fake display of power that he really didn't possess.

Give Hitler time, Friedrich thought dourly. Soon Hitler would control the world.

But that fact caused Friedrich to wonder about the British. Didn't they have anyone who could eliminate Hitler? Didn't England's new head of intelligence Bill Stephenson have the power and ability to assassinate Hitler if he tried? Stephenson, a man most of the world had never heard of, had recently been appointed by Winston Churchill as his informal and temporary chief of British intelligence. That appointment came after the Nazis completely compromised MI5 and MI6, Britain's once-reliable intelligence networks. Bill Stephenson was the new blood charged with the responsibility to clean up the mess.

If only Canaris and Stephenson would work together, Friedrich thought wistfully. Of course he knew that would only happen when the British stopped their appeasement of Hitler. That was the hope most thinking Germans were starting to hold.

Tonight might be an important time for Friedrich. Tonight he might be able to obtain more information about what Stephenson was likely to do, for in just a few minutes Friedrich would welcome one of Stephenson's private secretaries to his suite. Hopefully she might drop some information about Stephenson's plans.

But even better, she would drop more than that, Friedrich thought. They had been lovers for the last four years.

He must be ready for her.

Friedrich closed the drapes in his London hotel suite. Then he adjusted a painting on the wall that was slightly askew.

There. Now the suite looked more inviting. She would be here in only a matter of minutes. The thought crossed his mind about the deliciousness of anticipation. He often wondered if it wasn't even more magical than any *fait accompli.*

But enough speculation. Did he look acceptable? He assured himself of that, for he was well aware his tall, graceful stature permitted him to cut an impressive figure in those expensive clothes he always wore. He had also become adept in using his best feature, that rugged face of his with its lines and the nose with a slight hook, as an indicator of the exciting and adventurous life he must have led. How he could make those dark eyes flash with almost a manic sparkle when he wanted to.

And, as for his visitor who would soon arrive, by God he was ready for her. He smoothed the left side of his mustache, quivering at the thought that soon it would be she doing the stroking. He smiled at the thought that the sumptuous silk-covered bed, the elegantly upholstered chairs—all created a perfect spot for that stroking.

And joy of joys. She and he would have two full days alone before the Chamberlain reception was held to honor Joachim von Ribbentrop, the outgoing German Ambassador to the Court of St. James.

Friedrich had to smile at the realization of how frequently he referred to Sandra as She. He supposed that this was an unconscious recognition on his part of her ability to be an Every Woman for him. Even the thought of her could bring him to arousal when in his mind's eye he visualized her performing every sexual whim he had ever dreamed of.

But that was only part of the story. The wonderful part of all was the way she returned his ardor. In fact, he was aware that on many occasions her reactions to him outdid his ardor for her. At hearing that, she always flashed that happy smile he loved to see. "It's my 'throbs'," she said, referring to her own term for her prodigious ability to be aroused sexually.

"But I'm thirty three years older than you," he often jokingly protested, loving it when she responded that she could barely keep up with him in bed.

But she and he shared more than sex.

He had met her four years ago at a Bucharest embassy party while he was stationed there. Instantly he fell under her power, wondering if he had ever met anyone as lovely as she. Her eyes had a deep violet color to them that was electric when they looked into his. Her short, curly black hair tumbled carelessly around, serving as a frame for a face that one could stare at for hours. Hardly a moment of his life went by when he couldn't call up that face in his mind's eye. It was the perfect proportion her face possessed that astounded him. Those long cheek bones of hers perfectly positioned her nose so that every aspect of her face was in absolute proportion to the whole of it.

However, it wasn't always the face that beckoned him. Her body was exquisite. Although short, Sandra had a figure that was pleasingly full, much like a peach waiting to be sucked, as he once described it. Mentally he undressed that lovely body of hers at frequent moments during the day. In fact, it happened so frequently that he often had to stop himself before he went too far.

Loving her soon became his obsession. However, that love of his was also a protective one, for even though he regretted the necessity, he advised her that it was time for her to leave her job for Stephenson in Bucharest for security reasons. She should join Stephenson's staff in London. He would miss her very much, but he had no option but to do what was best for her. To ease the pain they had set up a private mail box so that they could write to each other every day. That's why he had jumped at the chance to attend this rather petty reception Chamberlain was hosting for Ribbentrop.

He checked his wrist watch. At that second he heard the slight sound of the key being inserted into the door lock. He swallowed nervously when the door begin to open slowly.

Bill Stephenson's secretary, born as Sasha Mardin in Romania, and now known in England as Sandra Martin, had entered Schulenburg's suite.

With an almost inarticulate gasp of joy, "Old Fitz," Sandra's nickname for Schulenburg, flung the door open. He carried her to a nearby chair where he placed her on her back and spread her legs wide. With one hand he lifted her skirt and pulled it back, leaving the other hand free to fondle the bare skin he found waiting for him. He had known it would be like this, for her boast to him was that she was always ready for him. With a moan of enjoyment, he thrust and as he did, she lifted her body to his, rubbing her nipples against his chest. She whispered to him in graphic details about the positions and the things she and he were going to do to each other's body.

And his response?

Beginning with the first item on her list of naughties, he proceeded to complete in order each item of a list that by now was etched in his brain.

Much later, she looked at him and laughed.

He looked at her with a puzzled expression.

"Is this how you greet everyone who comes to your door?" she asked.

"Only when it is you at my door."

She began to get up, but he pulled her back down on the bed and said, "Once more. Tell me what is your favorite on the list and we'll do it again."

"Wait," she said. She pulled out a capsule and split it in half, offering one half to him. "After this we'll never want to stop," she said.

"I'm too old---"

"I'll ignore that. We'll have time to recuperate before Chamberlain's reception for that idiot Ribbentrop."

He looked at her and shook his head. He had told her many times not to talk about important matters unless she was absolutely certain that no one could hear. Although he had checked this room for hidden cameras or tapes and had found it clean, he wanted her to be more careful. He wanted to learn more about Stephenson from her, but it would wait until they were outside and secure, he told her. It was a pity, for their bedroom conversations were always wonderful.

Importantly, he had warned her many times not to trust anyone with the facts about who Sandra Martin was. There were many influential Brits who would not tolerate having Sandra Martin, whose real name was Sasha Mardin, live in England. "If you ever need help, call me immediately. I'll always be there for you," he said.

"I know that," she said softly.

He regretted that he and she no longer lived in Bucharest, for he remembered the wonderful days that they had spent together when they'd driven along the dirt roads outside Bucharest. He could see in his mind the fields of ripening grain which lay next to dilapidated wooden cottages where fruit and vegetables hung drying in the air. Other products were sold by Romanian gypsies from their caravans. On days like this in Bucharest the two of them would often stop to savor the pungency of the air.

"You make me feel like the child I once was," he once said to her years ago, eager to rid himself of having to live in a world controlled by Nazis.

"You will always remain a child at heart, no matter who rules."

"And that might just be the death of me." He remembered how she had shivered in her heavy coat when he said that.

However, it was time to return from thinking about the past to the lovely presence of having her with him in this London suite. Memories were treasures that he could share at will with this lovely being.

She clung to him. "Come into the tub with me," she said, leading him into the bathroom where she ran the water very vigorously so that no conversation could be picked up if the suite were being taped.

She was going to Poland, possibly next week, she whispered to him while she washed his body. "I have some matters to attend to in Warsaw, and then Bill Stephenson wants me to go to the Krakow area. He won't tell me what for. Do you know of anything important happening in that area?" Friedrich shook his head. He would try to find out, though. "Is there a chance we could be together if I can change my current plans and meet you in Poland?"

"No," she said quickly. "I wish we could, but this trip has to be all business. How much longer do we have before Germany invades Poland?" He shrugged his shoulders. She had important business in Poland before that, she said. Even if he knew, she was aware that he would not tell her.

"Let's go back to bed," she said, her words heavily overlaid with sex. Her eyes filled with excitement while she looked at him with affection. He was a good lover, attentive and affectionate. But he couldn't compare with Walter. It was Walter who put her "throbs " into overdrive. And it was Walter who had promised to come to Poland for a short trip so that they could be together.

She rolled over and got closer to Friedrich so that she could explore his body with her fingers, all the while telling herself that the body she was touching was Walter's.

While all this was happening, multiple cameras located in strategic positions in each room of Friedrich's suite worked industriously. Every sound that Friedrich and Sandra created was captured, thanks to science's ability to sort background sounds from conversation or from the high-pitched sounds that sex creates.

"Every day," the engineers had been told before the project began. They were to provide written transcripts of all that occurred visually and vocally within that bedroom suite. "Every day," the voice warned.

Judging from the way that Sandra and Friedrich felt about each other, those pictures and transcripts should be explosive. What lucky person was going to receive such a great gift?

That was an interesting question.

Did the engineers have enough supplies to capture all of the activities of Friedrich and Sandra?

That was indeed an even more interesting question.

♦

Schulenburg was not the only person with Sandra Martin on his mind that day.

Ignace Chopa, leader of the resistance fighters in Krakow also was thinking about Sandra. However, his thoughts about her were not nice at all. In fact if he could, he would have made her disappear. But here he was on his way to a meeting with Sir Androz de Wiart. De Wiart, as he was known to all, was the leader of all the Poles who would eventually resist the Nazi takeover of their country. And that day was coming soon.

And what was their meeting to be about? War strategies? Battle plans?

No.

It was to be about Sandra Martin. The only reason Ignace was bringing this to De Wiart's attention was because Sandra was the daughter of one of de Wiart's closest friends.

"Is she still making passes at the resistance fighters?" asked de Wiart when Ignace mentioned her name. De Wiart had warned her about this several times.

"But it's worse than that. She has been boasting to everyone that the resistance will act soon to keep the Nazis from winning the war against us."

"Did she give any details about the action? Times? Places?" De Wiart was visibly upset.

"No. At least, not that I heard."

De Wiart breathed a sign of relief. Her actions in this instance had been wrong, but they weren't unfixable. "What we will do is move quickly into stage two of our plan. Emphasize to everyone that the action that we have planned will happen here in the Krakow area. That is important. But before you leave, get Sandra on the phone for me." De Wiart was glad that he had given orders to have Sandra under surveillance all the time.

When he heard her voice he told her exactly what he had told Ignace. "Is that clear, Sandra?" he asked.

When she agreed he hung up the phone quickly.

"Sandra," he muttered. She was becoming a liability. Suddenly that word triggered an idea. What a wonderful way to make Sandra an asset rather than a liability he thought as he turned the possibility around in his mind. Of course he would have to clear the idea first with Churchill. But he knew that would not be much of a problem. With one quick move he had removed her from his head and his heart. He was glad. That was what being a leader meant.

Chapter 3

Paul had to force himself to hurry on a day such as this.

He saw too many things on the campus to enjoy, like the variety of the stones in the walls that surrounded the colleges of Oxford or the endless variations of the color green in the velvet grass around him. But then, for him springtime in Oxford was always special. This day at Oxford University seemed much like the other lovely days Paul had encountered here years ago as a student. But his visit here today was for a far different purpose, however.

He traveled a gravel path, watching in fascination as the direct afternoon sun accentuated the colors of the leaves on the trees. On his left Paul saw the rambler roses that crowned the walls of the university houses. while on his right, the university playing fields still boasted the famous manicures that only English gardeners can produce. As for the weather, it was beautiful. Some early-morning fog that he had seen in London had rolled away and now in Oxford the air held a promising brightness. For Paul everything about Oxford became magic because of the place itself.

Paul loved Oxford. No matter how he might want to deny it, Andrei Novikov had been and still was a reason why that love existed. Their friendship was an old one, but one rooted at Oxford. It dated back to their first day as students when Andrei had stopped at the porter's office at Magdalen College to pick up his mail. A poorly dressed student standing outside the door had approached him. "Can you rent me one of your suite's extra bedrooms? Otherwise I'll have no place to sleep."

Paul was that boy.

Instantly liking him, Andrei took Paul back to his rooms for a cup of tea, and later, they worked out a living arrangement. Thus was born a friendship that lasted through the years since then and up to today. Andrei never suspected the truth, which was that the SIS had directed Paul to become friends with Andrei when they entered Oxford. After all, the nephew of the deposed Tsar might be a wonderful source for information about the allegiance of Russian expatriates in a world that being fragmented by the Nazis. But what difference did any of that that make, Paul reasoned, whenever the thought crossed his mind. Their friendship had always been legitimate, in spite of the fact that both men knew that Paul had loved Andrei's wife, Alexa, from the first moment he met her.

Paul snapped out of his reverie about the past to note how few students there were on campus today. With war looming, most students had probably given up on the academic life. After all, Paul reasoned, when you know that war will be declared soon and you face a strong possibility of dying in it, how much does anything else matter?

He regretted the dreary thoughts that were starting to dampen his spirits today. Perhaps his premonition that life would change because of the impending war was true. And perhaps the morbid thought of an Oxford bombed to smithereens by Nazi barbarians was not unrealistic. But truth and reality, although often sad, were also often happy, Paul decided. He must force his mind to retain its lovely memories of the past as well as to recognize the harsh realities of the present. Yes. He would try to do that.

He walked faster. He didn't want to be late for his appointment with Hugh Dalton, the man Churchill had directed him to meet. This was the man who would introduce him to the bitter English struggle against the Nazis that was soon to begin.

When he approached the college Paul recognized the college porter who was standing at the gates of Hugh Dalton's lodge as someone who had been there since Paul was an undergraduate.

"How are you, Jones?" Paul asked.

The porter's smile was the same as Paul remembered. "Just fine, Mr. Duke. Thank you. Mr. Dalton is waiting in his room for you. He just phoned down to ask if you had arrived. I'll tell him that you are here." Jones moved back into the lodge.

That done, Paul hurried into the quadrangle and began the climb to the room number Jones had given hm.

Hugh Dalton stood at the top of the stairs with the same excited "guess what" look on his face that Paul remembered from the past. Dalton had been at Oxford the same years as he and Andrei. They had never been friendly with him, but Paul attributed that distance to the seriousness with which Hugh attempted to convert everyone he met to Socialism. Since undergraduate days, though, Dalton had done well in his career. He followed up a doctorate in economics by authoring several important texts on Socialism as well as by entering politics as a member of Parliament from Camberwell.

"Come in, Paul," Dalton said, his voice just as notoriously booming as Paul remembered. That voice led Paul to recall what a recent writer in a leading magazine had said about Hugh. His meteoric career up the political ladder had been ascribed to his being a complete extrovert who loved the rough and tumble, as well as the shouting of a good fight.

That assessment troubled Paul. He disliked working with those who enjoyed the spotlight. They made things too risky, he thought. However, Paul would do exactly what Churchill had told him to do.

"Sit down," Dalton said, quickly removing books from a chair next to his desk. He handed Paul a glass of sherry. "I hope that it wasn't an imposition to ask you to see me here where I teach rather than at my office in London." His eyes stared at Paul. "I though this location would avoid prying eyes."

"Actually, I enjoyed the ride." Paul had been impressed that Dalton had provided for Paul's use a driver and a limousine to take him to and from the airport. The ride to Oxford had given Paul an opportunity to speculate about what his next assignment might be--as well as a chance to think about why Churchill had sent him to Dalton rather than to the director of the SIS, the person he usually reported to. Paul had heard rumors of trouble at the SIS, but he resolved not to mention his questions to Hugh. Not yet. It was too soon. However, at some point Paul wanted to know more about Hugh's place in all this. But at this moment all Paul wanted to do was bask in the joy of being at Oxford once again. It was Oxford's reverence for the past that he loved. Even Hugh's room was exactly the same as it was when Paul had been a student. Paul fumbled in his mind to express his reason for admiring the past. Guidelines, he decided. The past had the ability to bestow guidelines for where we had been and where we should be going.

"I haven't seen much of anywhere but Switzerland for the last year," Paul admitted. "Out with it, Hugh. Just what is happening here in England?"

Paul watched Hugh finish his sherry slowly before he spoke, as if he were making up his mind about something. Or perhaps he was debating about how to begin. While he waited for the man to begin, Paul observed the changes he now saw in Hugh. He was an older, more businesslike Hugh now, obviously shaped by what life was forcing him to accept. He seemed worried too, for while his fingers played with the stem of his glass, he spoke with care, a decidedly non-Hugh characteristic.

"You might yearn for the quiet of Switzerland again once you begin this next assignment,"

Hugh spoke with a rough laugh. "Churchill asked for you because you have the best credentials for heading up the project he has in mind. You are smart as well as able to succeed without anyone being aware that you are there. And you have been away from London for years. That's good. You haven't been identified with any particular side."

Hugh leaned back in his chair and swiveled while he was looking at Paul. "First of all, we don't want anyone here to know that you are involved in this particular project. No one. Is that understood? Something serious is at stake that involves a matter so important that it may determine the outcome of the war we face."

The room was still. Paul sat motionless at the words he was hearing.

"Let me answer some of your questions. Give you some of the "whys" and the "wherefores," Dalton said. "The reality is that very shortly Hitler will make his move against other countries. When he does, Great Britain will be in the middle of it. And, blast it, we are not prepared. Not by a long shot." Hugh looked out his window for a minute before he continued. "You are aware that when C, the director of the SIS died not long ago after a long illness, Prime Minister Chamberlain appointed Menzies to that position." Hugh sighed. "What a bad appointment that was."

Although Paul had few contacts with Menzies, he remembered the self-centered, rather dense man that Menzies had been. C had died shortly after directing Paul to move the Novikov household and himself from Paris to Zurich. At that time members of the SIS whom Paul had talked to thought that Menzies was a terrible choice for the post. The man had a reputation for acting impetuously without a careful examination of the facts.

"But let me back up a little," Dalton said. "Let me explain Churchill's role in all this."

Churchill was starting out with a disadvantage, thought Paul, but he wouldn't say that to Hugh. Before Hugh started, Paul said, "Churchill isn't about to win a popularity contest with the British upper class or with those who think we can keep Hitler in check by appeasement."

Dalton nodded. "Especially by the chief appeaser of all-- Prime Minister Chamberlain. As for the SIS, Churchill fought to have John Godfrey replace C after he died, but Chamberlain insisted on a temporary appointment for Menzies that turned out to be a disaster. Menzies has let the SIS go slack. Not only have SIS lines of communication been compromised, but because of the SIS's attempt to pacify him, Hitler has been encouraged to think that Britain will not fight."

Hugh stamped his fist in frustration. "Churchill is one of the very few leaders who understands the threat Hitler represents. But all everyone does is try to get rid of Churchill because of his honesty. And are those who do support Churchill organized? Of course not. We won't be able to build any defenses against Hitler until this country throws Chamberlain out and installs Churchill as prime minister. Hopefully, that should be soon. Up to now all that we have been able to do is set up an obscure agency called the Industrial Intelligence Center of the Committee of Imperial Defense, or the IICCID. That title is a mouthful, isn't it?"

"I've heard worse," Paul said evasively.

"We get no official money to function with. All we can do is collect information from anti-Nazis and from British servicemen who defy the Official Secrets Act by revealing to us how woefully underprepared our armed forces are for war. What we now realize is how important guerrilla warfare and terrorism will be for us when war begins. We certainly don't have guns and equipment to beat the Germans. But what we do have are loyal Brits who see the danger Hitler represents. That is where you enter the picture."

Paul waited for more information.

"Up to now we have relied on a group of patriotic Brits successful on the international level who want to use what they have learned to warn us of Britain's awful vulnerability to the Nazi menace. You will soon meet the most influential one of these men. He is Churchill's chief adviser, informally of course." He saw Paul's empty glass. "Another drink?"

When they were comfortable again, Dalton said, "The man you'll be meeting is William Stephenson. Have you ever heard his name?"

Paul shook his head.

"Bill Stephenson is a wealthy Canadian industrialist with business connections in many countries. After profits from his countless international companies began running into the millions of dollars, he diversified into other industries. Name an industry and chances are good that he owns much of it."

He went on. "For the past few years Bill has been providing confidential information to Churchill about Hitler's buildup of the army and how Germany's been hiding its military expenditures of eight hundred million pounds sterling. This is a clear violation of the Treaty of Versailles. But it shows the growing Nazi threat to European and international security. At the present time, Churchill is using Stephenson's information in Parliament to warn against the appeasement policies of the government of Neville Chamberlain. When and if war begins, Bill will probably establish and direct what Churchill wants to be a coordination office in New York to encourage the Americans to enter the war. "

“Where do I go from here, Hugh?” Paul asked. “What do you see as my role in this?”

“We want you to join us,“ Dalton said. ”As I told you, we have a specific job for you. However, before we go into that, Stephenson has an idea that he and I think might help you catch up on just where we stand. Prime Minister Chamberlain will host a farewell reception tomorrow in London in honor of Joachim von Ribbentrop who will be leaving his post as German Ambassador to the Court of St. James to become Hitler’s Reich Minister for Foreign Affairs. Key British governmental, political, and social leaders will be there as well as major German government officials. Stephenson would like you to attend and then meet with him later to share your observations and impressions about the current political climate.”

“That sounds like a good starting point,” Paul said.

“And after that, you will learn more about the assignment we have for you.”

“Will I be able to choose the members of the team who will work with me?” Paul asked.

“Of course. Go ahead and choose them.”

“Have you assigned anyone yet for my team?”

Dalton sat up straight at that question. “I assume that Stephenson will assign Sandra Martin to you, but he himself will explain all that to you.”

Paul realized it might be time to change the topic, since Hugh obviously was uneasy about telling him more. He turned to the topic of the upcoming reception. “Attending the reception will be helpful,” Paul agreed. However, he could also see problems in being publicly visible at the reception. “Will it be possible for me to go in disguise?” Paul asked.

Dalton saw no problem with that.

"Then this is what I will need." Paul scribbled a list of items and gave them to Dalton. "By the way, will the Ambassador from Canada be attending?"

"I suppose so."

"Make sure that he does attend and tell him that his economic attache will also be attending with him. That person will be me." Paul thought for a second, "Here's my new name. I'm Charles Scott Devereau from Montreal. By tomorrow, establish a Montreal address for me in case anyone checks up on me."

He and Dalton arranged Paul's schedule for the next few days. Then Paul left in the limousine for London and the safe house where he would stay during this trip.

The next phase of Paul's mission was beginning.

Hadn't it been Mariana who had described him as someone whom life couldn't change? He wondered about that. Perhaps change was good. At least, perhaps he needed change. He had held onto a hope for far too long that one day Alexa would love him. He despaired that this would ever happen. How much of his life had he given over to a dream?

Enough. It was time to put Alexa at the back of his mind and concentrate on the mission he was being given.

"Trust us," Dalton had asked of him.

No one could be trusted. Paul had learned that years ago, he reflected in the last few seconds before sleep swept over him that night. In one dream Alexa warned him not to undertake the mission Stephenson had for him.

"I can trust him," Paul answered Alexa in his dream.

"Are you sure?" countered Alexa. Paul swore that he could also hear Helena's laughter in the background whenever the word "trust " was used. He smashed his pillow onto the mattress. *I will make my life work. . . I will make it work.*

Chapter 4

Although the old cliché that opposites attract may be tired, it usually is true.

Just as it was true in this instance.

The two men who met here daily at the Tiergarten, Berlin's huge outdoor park, were high Nazi officials who feared each other's power, and yet would probably reluctantly admit to liking each other, or at the least, respecting the other's intelligence.

One was Rear Admiral Wilhelm Franz Canaris, Germany's head of the *Abwehr,* the country's Military Intelligence Unit, a position of great importance within the Nazi regime, for the *Abwehr* was tasked with the hunting out and destruction of all opponents to Hitler, among many other responsibilities.

Canaris was a brilliant military tactician who started his career during World War I. He soon became a hero for his exploits as a U-boat commander with 18 kills to his credit. He soon changed from the navy to military intelligence and created an excellent career in that field. Canaris was part of the regular German military establishment, a group that Hitler feared. And rightly so, for like Canaris, many of Germany's top officers opposed Hitler's moves to bring the country into another war and, like Canaris, were key members of a group of officers who secretly sought to depose Hitler as Germany's leader.

The other man in the Tiergarten that morning was *Brigadefuhrer* Walter Schellenberg of the *Schutzstaffel,* or the SS, the mention of which could create instant fear in the heart of every German, innocent or guilty. Schellenberg had recently become Heinrich Himmler's personal aide as well as deputy chief in the Reich Main Security Office under Reinhard Heydrich. Since Himmler held the position of general plenipotentiary to the whole Reich administration, Schnellenberg had enormous influence within Nazi Germany. His boss, Heinrich Himmler, was the second most powerful man in the Third Reich as well as the most ruthless. Himmler, with the assistance of Schellenberg, was currently in the process of initiating concentration camps.

Everyone in Berlin knew that each morning Carnaris and Schellenberg enjoyed some of their less stressful moments by meeting each other for a few minutes of conversation, usually in the nearby Tiergarten. Some mornings they would walk and on others they would take a horseback ride together in that huge city-center park almost equal in size to New York's Central Park. Then each would return to his office to deal with the "brain dead" who surrounded them. This last observation from Schellenberg to Canaris would, of course, be denied by Schellenberg if ever it became public, as would Canaris also deny that he had ever responded to Schellenberg by saying, "Few Nazis have any semblance of intelligence, present company excluded."

A strange pair, indeed, to share a friendship: the quiet, almost scholarly older admiral trained in the traditional Prussian aspects of war and the handsome, young, and above all, ruthless officer who was one of the rising new stars in the Nazi galaxy. Both of them were locked in a friendship as well as a competition. Schellenberg was a man who thrived in the dangers of the Nazi cult, as well as being a man of obvious perversions whose engrossing hobby was one of adding to his ongoing collection of pornography. As for Canaris, all he wanted at his core was to be loyal to Germany and to surround himself with his family.

But would each be loyal to the other if push came to shove?

Definitely not.

Canaris, for example, would probably define their relationship in hunter/hunted terms, seeing himself as the one hunted. Canaris always felt that Schellenberg was looking for proof of Canaris' anti-Hitler beliefs in order to prosecute him. That was very true. Schellenberg would have given everything he possessed to obtain hard evidence of what he knew Canaris had done. Just a few of these deeds involved supporting those who thought about assassinating Hitler as well as those individuals having a desire to act as peacemaker in order to avoid the future war.

But would Canaris also destroy Schellenberg if he had an opportunity? Most definitely, but only if such action also aided in destroying Hitler.

It could be said that their morning meetings had the ulterior purpose of being times when each could probe the other's weaknesses.

For Schellenberg, that meant finding the proof of Canaris' treason.

For Canaris, it was a time to find out how to shorten Hitler's hold on the country. Canaris believed that he knew the answer to that. Eliminate Schellenberg.

Walter Schellenberg must die. If he didn't die soon, Canaris would be uncovered as a traitor for his attempts to avoid war. and would be murdered. It was as simple as that.

The Tiergarten was usually empty during the early morning hours when they met, making it a good place to talk. Ahead of them the two men saw a quiet lake, silver blue in color, small in size, but completely surrounded by flowering birches. Canaris reined his horse to move backwards a few steps so that finally his face was parallel with Schellenberg's. He had something important to say during today's talk and he wanted to be in position to see the impact his information had on Schellenberg.

"Congratulations on how you staged the Venlo incident," Canaris began with a slight bow of the head. "It was quite clever of you."

"Thank you," Schellenberg said. "It really was, wasn't it?"

That was typical of Schellenberg, thought Canaris in admiration. Schellenberg was one of the few people he knew who honestly believed that everyone found him as superior as he believed himself to be. Canaris was momentarily jealous of such an ability. Although Canaris knew that Schellenberg's illusion was only a figment of his ego, he thought with envy of the many hours of self doubt it avoided for Schellenberg. Canaris, however, always maintained a distance from the world, a position he cultivated so that he might better survive the murky world of the spies.

As head of counterintelligence in early 1939, Schellenberg had conceived a plot against the British Secret Intelligence Service, the SIS, and two of its officers. These officers, Best and Stevens, were approached by a German double agent who pretended to represent a disaffected group of high-ranking anti-war German military officers.

These meetings culminated in what pretended to be an agreement to form a united German-British front against the Soviet Union after power was taken away from Hitler. The agreement included a period in which Hitler would be kept merely as a figurehead, and then after that, there would be a restoration of democracy and even legal protection for minorities such as Jewish citizens.

Not only were the talks a complicated German bluff, but the entire operation ended abruptly when Hitler decided to have the British operatives abducted at the beginning of the plot. However, by that time the Germans found on the agents not only damaging information about SIS secrets, but also a list of all the SIS agents in Europe.

"My plot showed the world that we Nazis mean business. Didn't it?" Schellenberg waited for Canaris' response.

"Of course."

"Careful, Wilhelm. Don't let your enthusiasm for the Nazi cause overwhelm you," said Schellenberg, his voice redolent with sarcasm.

"No fear of that. It never will," said the small, wiry Canaris, with the lisp that he was never able to control. It was time, decided Canaris. Now he would cast his net in front of Schellenberg and see what he could catch.

"Some unusual information came to me yesterday," Canaris began.

"From whom?"

Canaris smiled and went on. "I have a Polish source who is reliable. That source tells me that there is a lot of activity happening in the Polish area around Krakow. There is nothing definite to report, but a lot of Polish intelligence sources are suddenly showing up there. It seems to involve the death of a local resident. No one important, so I believe. However, guess who is nosing around the area?"

Schellenberg wasn't terribly interested so far. "Who?" he asked in a disinterested tone.

"Sir Androz de Wiart."

"Sweet Jesus," exclaimed Schellenberg. His voice spooked his horse who threw back its head and snorted. The sound reverberated and then disappeared. Schellenberg's mind started to try to put the information together. If de Wiart was involved, it was important, just as Canaris had said. He reached a fast conclusion. He must be the one who solved this, not Canaris.

"De Wiart is already a figure of legend for the British," Carnaris reminded Schellenberg..

De Wiart was indeed a Polish icon.

A British officer of Belglan and Irish descent, de Wiart won the Victoria Cross in World War I after having one eye shot out, losing his left hand, and biting off his left fingers when a doctor declined to remove them. At the end of World War I, he was sent to Poland as second in command of the British Military Mission there under Polish General Louis Botha. He later replaced Botha and became extremely sympathetic and helpful to the Polish cause in its battles with the Bolsheviks. Poles loved the man and would follow whatever he wanted them to do.

"I understand that de Wiart had just recently been recalled to his old job as head of the British Military Mission in Poland," said Canaris. "It is said that he never loses a battle."

"We'll see about that," said Schellenberg.

"I think that William Stephenson is also involved in this Krakow affair. Stephenson seems to have Churchill's ear so much that he is now directing English intelligence efforts," said Canaris.

"Only because of what I did at Venlo," boasted Schellenberg.

"Yes. Thanks to what you accomplished at Venlo."

Schellenberg made a quick decision. "I've changed my mind. I will attend the Chamberlain reception for Ribbentrop."

Canaris attempted to stifle a laugh.

"So what if von Ribbentrop is the world's biggest idiot? The reception may be the place to obtain information about what is happening in Krakow," Schellenberg said.

"Did you ever hear the story about how von Ribbentrop's elementary school teacher described him? She called him the most stupid student in the class, as well as full of vanity and very pushy," Canaris said. "That teacher was generous."

Schellenberg merely glared.

"Remember, my friend, that I am one of those fusty old members of the elite class that you hate. Von Ribbentrop is one of the new Nazi breed, so stupid that he can't be trusted to spell his own name correctly," said Canaris.

Schellenberg said nothing.

Enough teasing, Canaris thought. "I know that you will share with me anything you hear at the reception."

"Of course. Hasn't the Fuhrer often said that he wants our offices to cooperate with each other?"

This was too much for Canaris to swallow. "Walter, did you share the Venlo material with me? Didn't you want the credit for yourself?"

"Of course I did. But let me share something with you now. I will have someone deliver to your office today a file on William Stephenson that I want you to see."

Only what you want me to see will be sent, thought Canaris. "My dear Walter, my office also has a file on Stephenson that I will send to you today."

The two horses started stamping their hooves. They were anxious for the workout that was coming. When Canaris returned to his office later, he motioned for Hans Oster, deputy director of the *Abwehr*, to follow him outside the building for a short walk. When they were out of everyone's hearing Canaris told Oster everything that had happened in his meeting with Schellenberg.

"Good," said Oster. Canaris trusted Oster absolutely. It was Oster's mission from Canaris to develop the resistance movement against Hitler in Nazi Germany.

"Gisevius is already on his way to London for the Chamberlain reception," he told Canaris. Gisevius, also on Canaris' staff, had been named as chief of special projects by Canaris. In this position he and Oster would work secretly to overthrow Hitler. It was the ultimate hope of Canaris to send

Gisevius to serve as Nazi military intelligence officer in the German consulate in Zurich next year.

"I want you to follow Schellenberg very closely. I want to know all the people he associates with." Canaris thought he already knew the answer to this, but there was no harm in collecting direct proof. He was pleased with what he had accomplished. The chase was indeed afoot.

♦

Nearby, optimism was not quite the order of the day when Walter Schellenberg returned to his office Had Canaris really obtained information about de Wiart being in the Krakow area or was this a typical blind for a trick that Canaris planned? But he would get answers, he vowed.

"I want a plane to London right away," Schellenberg directed his aide. "Five agents will be going with me." He would get to the bottom of this quickly. He was well aware that war turned every one into both victims and executioners. But not him. He would never become a victim.

And at the same time the trip would give him time with Sandra in London. In addition to sex he would find out if she knew of anything happening in the Krakow area. God, he was fascinated by her. She had the ability to keep him excited all the time whenever he thought about her. If she were pure German he would have married her without a doubt. He dismissed the spying which she did for Stephenson and the Allies, for all of it was usually petty material that he could easily get from other sources. As for her sex life, Walter was certain that she had slept with half the important men in Europe and England. But he could end that whenever he wanted to. To be truthful, her sex life with others fascinated him. As for what he would do with her when war began, he hadn't figured that out yet. But he didn't want to give her up. He knew that for a fact.

♦

At that moment De Wiart had taken a few minutes that morning to sit and think about Sandra and about the plan that he had put together with her as a linch pin.

He realized that in a way everything revolved around Sandra. De Wiart was certain that he had correctly gauged Walter's feelings for Sandra, as well as her feelings for Walter. And most importantly, Sandra's feelings for him. To be honest, de Wiart was bored pretending to be Sandra's loving uncle, particularly if the nymphomaniac was beginning to interfere with his plans for winning the war against Hitler.

It all would come together. De Wiart was confident that he could control Sandra's every move. In doing that he would also give himself, and others, like Canaris, the pleasure of seeing Walter destroyed.

Chapter 5

Well before the time specified on the invitations, the driveway to the building in London's Whitehall district began filling with a procession of elegant cars. All of these seemed anxious to deposit their impatient passengers at the farewell lunch reception which Prime Minister Neville Chamberlain was hosting for Joachim von Ribbentrop, the outgoing Ambassador to Germany who had just received an appointment from Hitler as Germany's Foreign Minister.

Out of the cars stepped a variety of people.

Those who were English-speaking ranged from the highest lords of the land to leading governmental figures such as Winston Churchill and his wife and the United States Ambassador to England Joseph P. Kennedy and his wife, and finally, to the rank and file employees of the embassies housed in London.

Also included were an array of Nazi sympathizers, artists, filmmakers, and of course foreign correspondents from countries large and small, all dressed in the latest fashions. And finally among the always last-minute arrivals were the German State Secretary, Bernhard von Bulow; German Foreign Minister Neurath; French Ambassador Francois-Poincet; Sir Eric Phipps, the British Ambassador, and Count Friedrich-Werner von Schulenburg, the German Minister to Russia.

Paul and his party hesitated for a moment at the doorway, almost like skiers waiting their turn as they readied themselves to be introduced to their host and hostess. Prime Minister Chamberlain and his wife stood at the entrance to the ballroom, waiting to greet each new arrival. Outwardly Chamberlain was behaving as he always did at such affairs, hiding what Paul felt was nervousness with ironic quips, his expression always that of a skeptic ready to laugh at what he viewed.

After the Chamberlains greeted them, Paul and his party, which included Canadian Ambassador to England William Perry and his wife, were escorted by white-gloved aides to an elegant reception room to feast on cocktails and hors d'oeuvres. For this event Paul was dressed as a rather pudgy Canadian Embassy minor official whose name was Charles Scott Devereau of Montreal. The Canadian party was neither the first or the last to enter, since Paul thought it wise never to be the first or the last to arrive at anything if one wished to be unobserved. He straightened the collar of his black suit that deliberately was one size too small for him and of a style that had gone out of fashion several seasons ago.

Hugh Dalton had done a great job of providing props for Paul, and quickly, too. "Choose a Canadian friend of yours who is an Ambassador or a high embassy figure and is going to the Chamberlain reception," Paul had requested before the two of them left Oxford. The Canadian official should introduce Paul as a low-level member of his staff.

"Please tell me some facts about who I am so that I can read it before the reception," Paul requested.

That accomplished, Paul and Hugh had stopped before the reception at the London hotel suite that Hugh had provided for him to get dressed. It took time, but Paul squeezed himself into the small suit. His transformation was complete with a borrowed pair of non-prescription glasses. A heavy layer of hair jell was perfect for making him look like a poor man's Rudolph Valentino.

"My own mother wouldn't recognize me," Paul said after he looked into the mirror.

"I sincerely doubt that she would want to," Hugh said very honestly.

♦

Ambassador Perry adhered carefully to the information he had been given in his briefing by Hugh. He was to concentrate on circulating widely around the groups and then speaking briefly to acquaintances. Also, if possible, he was to avoid bringing his consular staff members into conversations. Paul wished to merely listen to what was being said and to quietly observe what was happening.

Paul did just that. It worked. In retrospect, the von Ribbentrop reception provided lots of disparate information that he would later have to sort through. Although von Ribbentrop was acknowledged by all who attended as having, as one Nazi whispered to another, the intellectual capacity of a tse-tse fly, "Champagne Charlie," as the pretentious one-time wine merchant was called by all, was a handsome, amiable, fun loving soul who never sufficiently understood the implications of anything he heard. Thus he never was a menace to anyone. Everyone invariably assumed that whatever Ribbentrop said had the possibility of being a falsehood, whether intentional or accidental.

The Churchills were a couple that seemed uncomfortable, at least, they were uncomfortable each time Paul looked their way. Paul wondered if it was because Churchill saw all the aides who were from time to time quietly conveying whispered messages to Chamberlain, today's host.

"Probably messages that German troops are marching into Austria as we speak in order to make it part of the German Reich," Ambassador Perry whispered grimly to Paul.

Uncertainty did seem to be in the air at the luncheon, with everyone speculating about how close the world was to war.

"Those messages Chamberlain is receiving should make Joe Kennedy happy," Paul answered in disgust. He stared at the American Ambassador whose public declarations always approved Chamberlain's attempts to appease Hitler. Paul wondered if Roosevelt was aware of the damage that Kennedy's words could cause at a time when every public action of a diplomat was important in assessing the words of one's enemy. Hitler probably believed that his aggression would go unnoticed or even be approved, if one listened to an appeaser such as Kennedy.

When Chamberlain replaced Stanley Baldwin as prime minister in 1937 he continued Baldwin's policy of nonintervention. Chamberlain believed that Germany had been badly treated by the Allies in World War I and thought that war could be averted by agreeing to some of the demands being made by Hitler and Mussolini. Lord Halifax, Chamberlain's foreign secretary, fully supported Chamberlain's policy.

After the reception Paul and Ambassador Perry managed to position themselves around specific people. One of these was Colonel Hans Oster, the man Hugh Dalton identified to Paul as Canaris' deputy at the *Abwehr* and an opponent of Hitler. Paul imagined how disappointed Oster must have been to hear all the talk about appeasement at the luncheon. Especially so, Hugh had said, since not long ago Oster had received a message of support from Ewald von Schmenzin, an important member of the German nobility. It said, "If England is willing to fight, we shall end this regime." Knowing the extent of English appeasement, Paul had been told that Canaris had crumpled the paper in disappointment. To men such as Canaris and Oster, today's reception must certainly be proof that Great Britain had no intention of trying to stop the Nazis.

However, most of the English present today were loyal to their country, no matter how skewed their ideas about appeasement might be. One disagreement did break out however, about whether Edward VIII had been a traitor to his country, for Edward, during his brief time as king, had made no secret of his approval of the Fuhrer. As someone mentioned, hadn't Churchill seen a subsequent letter from Hitler to the Duke of Windsor after his abdication? It said that in exchange for his support, Hitler would return Edward to the throne when it was possible for him to do so.

However, some members of the English aristocracy at the reception, such as Lady Emerald Cunard, did openly mention their support of Hitler's cause. Why wouldn't she be open about it? After all, Paul was in the group at the luncheon who heard Joseph Kennedy describe Chamberlain in public as the "greatest man after the Pope." And also, hadn't Paul heard Unity Mitford, the English woman rumored to be one of Hitler's mistresses, say how great a savior Hitler was for Germany?

Paul also winced as he listened to Lord Halifax tell a group how much he supported Hitler's claim just a few days ago that "the German race represents the highest evolution of the human species." To add insult to injury Halifax had also remarked to another guest at the luncheon that it was "unthinkable" that the Third Reich not be allowed to expand its living space. Another Englishman who should have known better, Sir Arthur Rucker, Chamberlain's principal private secretary, was heard to say that Communism was a greater danger to Great Britain than Nazi Germany.

No wonder thought Paul that Churchill looked uncomfortable today.

Of course the Nazis at the luncheon felt absolutely no quibbles at criticizing what the world was doing to them.

Paul overheard the lament of one tall handsome Nazi officer who said very loudly, “It is very sad for a German to find how misjudged and abused his country is. Of course our enemies control the press in foreign countries, and they have been very busy. They have clever tongues and they lie.”

Paul steered Ambassador Perry away for a private question. “Who is that lying German idiot?”

“That is Walter Schellenberg, the ambitious deputy chief of the German foreign intelligence section. He is no idiot, nor should you ever assume that he is. Schellenberg is one of the smartest and most dangerous Nazis that there are.”

At one point during the afternoon when guests were beginning to say their goodbyes, Paul turned his attention to William Stephenson, the man at the center of a group off to one side of the room. Although the man seemed to be the center of the group’s attention, Paul found the man’s face rather unprepossessing, although if you analyzed each feature of his face individually each was pleasing or at least average. It was just that the face was unremarkable at best. Perhaps that was it, Paul decided. Stephenson might be one of those people who prefer a face-free identity. Paul conceded that this was often helpful in intelligence work.

“Walk with me over to that group so that I can talk to that man, will you?” he asked. Ambassador Perry.

“You mean Bill Stephenson?”

Paul nodded. Somehow he had guessed that this was who it was. He thought that it might be expedient to speak casually to Stephenson, the man to whom he would soon report. But Stephenson’s attention was elsewhere. It clearly rested on a lovely young woman with extraordinarily light violet eyes who was dancing by herself, moving from person to person in the group, demonstrating a new dance step, or so she said. Certainly it was a dance step that afforded her the opportunity to have others stare at her, thought Paul. He wondered about her. She seemed unable to control, let alone modify her feelings. Those feelings of excitement reflected in her face at being the center of attraction seemed to him to betray the emotions of a passionate inner life. Her cheeks were flushed with joy. He wondered if passion were the recurring pattern of her life.

"Who is she?" Paul asked.

"She's Sandra Martin, a secretary within one of Stephenson's many corporations based here in London. Lovely, isn't she?"

She was lovely, Paul decided, but certainly no one he admired. Frankly he found her type worrisome. She depressed him and inextricably filled him with a sense of foreboding. To be honest, he always found extreme beauty to be intimidating and confusing at the same time. Experience had shown him that any beautiful woman usually fell into one of two categories. Either she had been placed here on earth by the gods to be an oracle who illustrates perfection to mortals, or she was a robotic shell sent to deceive mortals into believing that beauty also brings with it the ability to think. Paul would bet that rather than expecting the words of an oracle, one should expect a spirited discussion of style to emanate from Sandra's mouth.

"And the older man next to her who is trying to get her attention?" Paul knew that that man didn't find the woman confusing. Rather, he was panting for her body.

The Ambassador smiled. "That is Count Friedrich-Werner von Schulenburg, a known womanizer as well as a loyal member of Germany's military elite."

As for Stephenson, Paul's quick look grudgingly evaluated him as personable, at best. Dig past that crust layer of civility and Paul wondered what one would find the man to be made of. Paul happened to catch a look of suspicion on Stephenson's face while Stephenson was looking at Sandra. Paul wondered what it meant.

♦

Ambassador Perry introduced his group and then introduced Paul, using the fake name Hugh Dalton had given him for the reception.

Paul was about to ask Sandra to dance with him when the string quartet stopped.

"Sorry," he said to her. "I have that annoying habit of always being late."

"Next time start earlier," she said. "I want to dance with you." Her laughter had an infectious ring to it.

After that, the luncheon guests said their goodbyes to each other and scattered.

When he reached the street outside, Paul saw the same lines of limousines that he had seen earlier. Waiting would take forever, he decided. He discovered that he was slightly down about what he had seen and heard today. Perhaps by walking he could eliminate some of the bad taste the reception had left in his mouth. On a whim he said goodby to Ambassador Perry and started walking. He would walk until a taxi passed by for him to hail.

Then he saw her.

Sandra Martin was only about half a block ahead of him. If he hurried he could catch up to her.

"Remember me? It was your advice that I start earlier if I wanted to keep up with you," he reminded her when he arrived at her side. "May I walk with you and possibly entice you into stopping for a drink? You do owe it to me, you know. To make up for my lost dance."

"Aggressive, aren't you? Canadian, right? Well, I'd like you to walk me home. But home is only about three blocks away. I'd invite you in for a drink, but I have a meeting at Whitehall only an hour from now and I can't be late for it." She did seem genuinely sorry.

"Then let's get started," he said. He put her arm in his and started a fast walk.

He saw that she liked his energy and his willingness to go after what he wanted. Good. He had thought that she would like that approach. "I heard that you are Stephenson's secretary?"

She nodded, obviously not interested in telling him too much about herself.

He would try another approach.

"Lots of damned German sympathizers at this luncheon today. I don't know how you feel, but they made me sick."

He saw that she was attempting to look interested in what he was saying. "Sick?" she repeated. Her voice had some passion in it, but not much. "They make me sick, too. As Mr. Stephenson's secretary I can't show my dislike for Nazi doctrine in public, but it's there, I can assure you."

But was it? Her guarded words made it difficult to decide just who was the real Sandra. Whose side was she on? He was willing to bet that a broken fingernail would elicit more passion from her than a discussion about appeasers.

She stopped in front of a semi-detached home on Cheyne Walk. "This is where I live." She looked at him apologetically. "Another time, perhaps?"

Paul nodded. "I'll be back in London in about two or three weeks. I'll contact you as soon as I can."

She ran up the steps.

Something--intuition, experience—call it what you will, told Paul to circle the service drive in the back of the crescent of homes where Sandra lived. He found that there was a thick concentration of shrubs on the right side which would shield him from view but afford a good view of anyone who approached her house from the front.

He would hunker in for a stay. It would probably be a waste of time, but then, it might not.

After fifteen minutes his dedication began to waver. And too, the smell of cat pee that emanated from the bushes was starting to gag him. Just then a black limousine with a German diplomatic license plate whipped around the corner to stop in front of Sandra's building. Instantly Sandra opened the front door of the building where she lived and quickly descended her front marble steps.

A Nazi guard jumped out of the front passenger's seat in the car and opened the back door for Sandra. Although Paul had only a brief look, it was enough to see that it was Walter Schellenberg who had reached across the back seat and kissed Sandra before the door closed and the limousine sped off.

Obviously this was not one of those Nazis whom Sandra had labelled as "sick." The question was clear. Given Sandra's passionate nature, just how did she feel about Schellenberg?

♦

It did not take Paul much brisk walking through London to reach the Royal Falcon Pub after he left his hiding place behind Sandra's flat.

There were two entrances to the building. One, the one Paul used, led to an upstairs flat while the other opened into the pub. Catering to the upscale Whitehall governmental neighborhood, its kitchen offered wonderful pub food. Most important of all, the pub was owned by a very special person. Harry Paine had been Paul's partner at the SIS for many years.

Paul had called Harry, the pub's owner, this morning to schedule this meeting. The friends shook hands and walked to a large booth. After giving Paul a quick look the group at the bar turned back to their drinks. "After you explained that you had been summoned by Bill Stephenson, I thought it would be helpful if I invited another person to this meeting," Harry said. He looked at another chair facing a fireplace on the far side of the room. "Come over here, Dave," he said.

Dave Christie got up and walked to their table.

As old friends do, Paul stood up and put his arm around Dave's shoulder. "SIS doesn't have anyone like you and Harry anymore, Dave. Thanks for being here." The three of them had always worked well together; however, they had also remained as personal friends through the years.

The son of English parents, Dave Christie had lived in Germany for years. Recruited by the SIS for work in Germany, it had been Christie who met with Hermann Goering and learned in 1938 of Germany's plans to take control of Austria and Czechoslovakia, even discovering the specific days the takeovers would occur. However, the British government refused to believe Christie, just as it chose to disbelieve his information that Hitler could be ousted by the German military if and when Britain joined forces with Czechoslovakia to fight Hitler.

As a result, Christie's career had been destroyed. "Harry is helping me to build a new life in business," Dave explained. "The present SIS cannot be trusted. We must wait until Churchill becomes prime minister to get British intelligence operating again."

Paul told Dave and Harry what Dalton and Churchill had told him. He talked about the upcoming meeting that he would have with Stephenson within days. "I will share with you both what I learn," he promised. He also told them that they were on the payroll again. "In the meantime, will the two of you get me some information that I will need when I meet with Stephenson?"

He explained what he needed and then they arranged to meet the next night. "Can we trust Stephenson?" he asked them.

Christie paused and then summarized the situation as he saw it, although Paul had already known part of what Dave said. However, since it was important to have confirmation from people Paul trusted he did not interrupt them as they spoke. ”There’s been a major shift in the SIS. Because Churchill can’t trust it anymore, he has turned to Bill Stephenson.to run intelligence temporarily. Stephenson is a wealthy Canadian who has been appointed to head up the British Security Corporation (BSC) out of New York City. This is an umbrella organization that is in the process of overseeing all the British intelligence agencies—MI5, SIS, and all the rest.”

“And?”

“And Stephenson is the only man whom Churchill trusts to head it up.”

“What happened to SIS?” Paul asked.

Harry took a deep breath before he began. “When Churchill returned to the Admiralty he became a victim of verbal abuse from both Berlin and Parliament. When Admiral Sir Hugh Sinclair of SIS died, Chamberlain wanted Stewart Menzies to become the permanent new chief. But Churchill feared that Menzies was letting SIS become careless. Menzies was more afraid of the Bolsheviks than the Nazis.”

“And?” asked Paul.

“It gets worse.”

“How?” asked Paul with a sinking feeling in his stomach.

Harry explained his version of the Venlo Incident to Paul. When he finished, Dave said, “It was Menzies, Chamberlain’s choice, who allowed his two agents to walk into the trap.”

Paul said, “Let me get this straight. The SIS now has no way of communicating with its agents. And its stupidity is responsible for the death of two agents. Right?”

Harry nodded.

There was a silence and then Paul spoke. "Churchill has placed all our intelligence under Stephenson?"

"Temporarily," said Hugh. "He's all we've got. He's a self-made man who has become phenomenally wealthy because of his own efforts. He's smart. I'll say that for him."

Paul mentioned all the pro-Nazi appeasement drivel he'd just heard today. "Churchill is going to have a hard fight. I meet with Stephenson soon. I need to know more about him." Paul also mentioned Sandra Martin, noting that she seemed to be a good friend of Stephenson. "I don't trust her. Can you get me information about her and her background?"

"We're ready to start," said Dave. Harry nodded his head.

They had confirmed what Dalton had told Paul. And that was important to him. They talked for a while longer before everyone left quietly and separately. Downstairs the pub was starting to swing into its late afternoon slightly high hilarity mode. For a second. Paul momentarily longed for the opportunity to share a good laugh with someone. But he had too much to do. *I always have too much to do,* he noted sourly.

♦

Later that evening Paul took a few minutes to sit and think about today. He had listened to a variety of viewpoints about how to deal with Hitler. The dark matter of Nazi Germany was threatening to reshape the very structure of life for the world. In any restructuring Paul always feared most those who enjoy danger for its own sake, as opposed to those who fight for ideas. These danger seekers were the ones who, like the exquisite violet-eyed Sandra Martin, dance around event horizons of black holes for the fun of it. However, she was also one of those who by her blind attractiveness often would suck others into a black hole of nothingness from which there would be no escape.

Would the world get its act together and fight as a unit against the Nazis as soon as Hitler began his offensive? Paul despaired that it wouldn't. *We share this world. We make laws together to enhance this world. We discover the beauties of this world. But by never exploring the needs of every heart with which we come in contact, we, too, circle our own black holes,* he decided.

For his part, he was afraid that the world was unable to work together. Hitler would seize power. And then the entire world would have to fight, and at a time when Hitler had become very strong. Better to meet the threat now, Paul thought, rather than later.

But the world was not always led by logic, as he well knew.

♦

Walter Schellenberg opened the packet which an aide brought to him in the office provided for him at the German Embassy in London. It was early evening and Walter was tired. It had been a busy day for him.

"Thank you," he said to the aide who saluted and left. When the man was gone, Schellenberg got up and went to the door and locked it. He returned to his desk and reached into his briefcase which sat beside the desk. Yes, he had remembered to pack his magnifying glass for this trip to London. Slowly he pulled each photo out of the packet and arranged them carefully according to poses on the top of his desk. The shots in which Schulenburg lay on top of Sandra or vice versa were the ones he automatically discarded. There wasn't much to see in those. The other photos, of which there were many, intrigued him. Sandra was a beautiful woman, although he had seen many just as lovely. But sexually, she was outstanding. It was as if she had been born for sex. He expanded the phrase—*born for the bed.* That would be the title of the section devoted to Sandra in his scrapbook. He thought about that. He might have enough good shots of Sandra with him and others to dedicate an entire scrapbook to her. He'd see about that. And Schulenburg had given him some good ideas about positions and activities that Walter decided to try with Sandra the next time that they were together. As for Sandra—Sandra looked happy no matter what Schulenburg did to her. Nor what any man did to her, Walter thought. Was he jealous of the many who had slept with her? Of course not.

Switching topics, Walter thought about his most recent time alone with Sandra. Screwing aside, Sandra had seemed truthful when she said that she knew nothing about anything happening in the Krakow area. But he told her how to check on that in her upcoming trip, and she promised to try to get more information for him when she was in Krakow. He had to admit that she hadn't been enthusiastic about what he wanted her to do, but Walter had ways to ensure that she would do as she was told.

By now he was determined at any cost to unlock the secret which Canaris had alluded to the morning of their riding session. The Fuhrer would see how Walter could succeed where Canaris failed. He must find the military plans in Krakow. And it was Sandra who was going to help him immeasurably, he decided, irrespective of how little she might want to help him.

♦

Back in Berlin, Admiral Canaris, like Walter, was also strategizing. However, Oster's evaluation of the recent von Ribbentrop reception depressed him. What cowards the British were. They couldn't understand that if they stood up to Hitler right now, right now, that is, they could beat him.

However, a noose was being tightened around Schellenberg's neck. *If only Schellenberg's ego pulls him into the trap*, thought Canaris. *Let it work,* he prayed.

Chapter 6

Sandra almost flew up the steps to her apartment building on Cheyne Walk after her meeting with Walter. In spite of her trembling hands she managed, but just barely, to unlock her door.

Once inside, though, she ran out of energy and leaned against the door, taking deep breaths until she had calmed down. It seemed to her that at that moment all of the rest of her life suddenly disappeared, as if what she was feeling now was reality and everything else around her, including all her past, had only been an illusion or, at best, a dream. She despaired that everything in life had lost its significance for her.

Shakily she lit a cigarette and sat down on the sofa to think about what had happened earlier tonight while she was with Walter. She always was able to remember every moment that they had spent together and she always would. But why did it have to turn sour? She feared that this was the question whose answer would always depress her.

As usual, she and Walter made time for sessions of lovemaking whenever they were in town together, just as they had done tonight after the von Ribbentrop reception. She remembered the moments of pleasure and happy anticipation they had shared tonight. It started when the chauffeur was helping her into the car to sit beside Walter so they could drive off to their secret apartment. Walter's leg had touched hers briefly and then quickly moved. *Later,* was the implicit promise of that touch. *Later* when we are alone. *Later* when we are at the apartment. Not that much later, the promise of that touch was fulfilled.

After that always came moments of pure joy for her. Usually it was when Walter sat up in bed and looked at her with a satisfied smile that managed to soften the slightly severe look that was usually on his handsome face. She regarded its lack of vulnerability as one of the beauties of his face.

It seemed to her an indication of how well the owner knew himself and her. Today his elbow playfully poked her breast.

"Get dressed," Walter said softly. "We need to talk. It is impossible for me to think straight with your naked body touching me."

Soon they were sitting on the sofa together. He and she had known each other for over a year, and although the sexual attraction between them had been strong from the moment they met, her mind had never considered him as anything but a Nazi and therefore ineligible for any part of her heart. Thus she took their sex life for the fantastic thing it was. As for their political views, she had no hesitation in letting him know how much she disliked the Nazis. At the beginning of their affair she had hoped he wanted a relationship that was solely about them. But increasingly she was beginning to realize that this would soon be impossible. The more she learned about what Hitler planned, the more she despaired. The end of their relationship might soon be coming for Walter and her. The sadness she felt at this surprised her by its intensity. However, try as much as she could, she could envision no way of postponing the breakup of their affair. She had no intention of being drawn into something where he used her for political reasons. Nor would she do that to him.

"I want to talk about you, Sandra," he began, his voice displaying what she always laughingly labeled as his lapse into Teutonic twaddle.

It caught her attention, though. Here it comes, she thought. It was going to be Walter, not her, who broke off their affair.

But that wasn't his topic at all.

"I know enough about your life to know how much danger you will face in the war that is coming. Your background will destroy you. And that war is coming quickly," he said. "You hate the Germans. I accept that, merely remarking in my defense that all sides in a war are always cruel. I predict that you will work beyond your endurance for the Brits and the Allied cause, but mark my words, when it is to their advantage they will betray you. I have something here to show you." He reached over to his jacket and extracted an envelope, taking out a picture that was inside. It was a family photograph of her father and mother and her mother's father and mother.

"I know that you have Jewish blood," he whispered.

His words were a shock to her. She had kept the truth as a closely guarded secret that she thought only Bill Stephenson and Schulenburg knew. Or so she had thought.

He said, "But I do understand what it is like today to have Jewish ancestors. As for you, you were born in Bucharest, Romania, the only daughter of Max Rosenberg, a German Jew who as a young man prospered in the South African diamond trade. He later moved to Romania in 1902 to invest with other family members and to begin a flourishing empire in furs and timber." He looked carefully at her. "Your mother was also a Jew, wasn't she?"

She nodded. Her mother was Hilda, daughter of Heinrich Marin, who had fled Russian anti-Semitic pogroms and settled in 1874 in South Africa where he promptly shed his Jewish name for the safe one of Martin. His daughter, now named Hilda Martin, became the wife of Max Rosenberg in a London synagogue in 1902.

Sandra always became bitter when she thought about her mother. She looked at Walter and said, "My mother was ashamed of her background. For her entire life she never spoke of her Jewish background, although she enjoyed the fact that her husband became an extremely wealthy man who counted as his friends the members of Romanian nobility. It was Hilda's hope, which she has by now achieved, I might add, of one day living in a British village. My mother was also responsible for my new name. Little Sasha Marin is known by my new name of Sandra Martin."

"Do you want to hear more than that?" she asked with a sadness in her voice. Walter fondled her arm when she continued at his insistence. "Max traveled a great deal in his work, which was an advantage for him since it gave him time for his secret occupation, which was to assist Jewish survivors of anti-Semitism to reach Israel through Romanian ports. His money managed to bribe many border guards."

"Max must have been an interesting man," said Walter. "How about your mother?"

"I have little use for her," she said tersely.

Actually, as Walter well knew, for he had researched the Rosenberg family history, the truth was reversed. It was Hilda who had little time for little Sasha. With all her clothes shopping, hobnobbing with Romanian duchesses, buying furniture for her mansion on the Danube, and aping the habits of British society, Hilda spent little time with the three Rosenberg children, Sasha, Sasha's younger brother Wilfred, and her older brother, Ralph. During their youth in Romania the Rosenberg children lived a happy life without Hilda, for they were permitted to roam at will outdoors with the children of Romanian peasants as well as the Romanian gypsy children who would do anything that the Rosenberg children requested, once they provided food or money.

"Let me tell you something interesting, Walter. You might even find it worthy of being in one of your albums." He had told her about these a long time ago, although she hadn't seen one. He smiled at her words. "Tell me and I'll let you know."

She spoke slowly at first as she began her story.

"By chance my father Max returned home early one time from an extended trip on the Danube. He found my brother Wilfred sitting in tears at the bottom of the dirt road that led up to the Rosenberg mansion. I was about eight, at the time, I think."

"What is wrong?' Max.asked.

"It is Ralph's fault," Wilfred said with a sob. "He won't let me in the coach." Wilfred was referring to a nearby gypsy encampment that included some empty coaches for storage.

According to Wilfred, Ralph had made him pay to enter, just like all the other boys did if they wanted to play.

"But why?" wailed Wilfred to Max. "She's my sister."

Max let out a roar and raced to the coach where he found what he feared. At least 12 boys were lined up inside waiting their turn with a rather dirty but happy and naked Sasha. Ralph was obviously the time keeper as well as the entrepreneur for the project, since there was a pile of pennies which he jealously guarded.

Sandra went on. "I remember turning to my father and boasting that it was a new game that Ralph taught us. And it was fun."

"See? You've always been fun,'" said Walter.

"Hush," said Sandra. "Let me continue. When the local doctor arrived not long after at the Rosenberg mansion he was asked to examine me and after that, he began to set Ralph's nose. As for my mother, Hilda, she had the beginnings of a black eye which she said she had gotten from bumping into a door in a dark room."

"Her eye doesn't need treatment," Max assured the doctor. "She must learn to be more careful in the future," Max said as he looked at Hilda.

"That's my story," concluded Sandra. "As for my brother Wilfred, he never forgave Ralph for not being able to play that game. After that, Max threatened Hilda. He also hired a nanny, one of whose tasks was to guard the safety of the children, particularly me, Max's favorite child. Many were the nights when I would creep into the bedroom where Max slept by himself and crawl up next to him. Max tried to make up for not always being around. He hired the best horsemen to teach me to ride, as well as the best marksmen to teach me to use a gun, and the best dance instructors to teach me social graces."

Sandra interrupted her story by pulling Walter's head down to her breast. She said, "Max counseled me as well. He warned me that sex was Bucharest's chief preoccupation."

"He was right," Sandra continued. "I found out early that sexual intrigue was part of the Romanian picture—the spies, the daggers, the lies of living in an area whose abundant reserves of oil would soon be sought by those who would fight the oncoming war. When I was old enough, Max sent me to a finishing school in Switzerland. After that I was ready for the real world."

Walter looked at her. "That 'real world' started for you in Bucharest, didn't it?"

"Yes," she said softly. "Did you know that Bucharest is called the 'Paris of the East' by those who know its importance to the world?"

"I know," he said. "It was in Bucharest that you became a spy for England, wasn't it?"

There it was. The word "spy." The word that she never wanted to hear. Was she a spy? Not up to now she wasn't. After all, the mere tidbits which she received from sex-besotted men such as Schulenburg could probably have been gotten from many sources. At least, that was what she told herself. But what about the war that was coming? Information during wartime would be more than "mere tidbits." Information would be facts that would result in the death of many people, even oneself.

Was Walter going to ask her to spy for him? She was afraid that he was. That, of course, would end their relationship earlier than she had planned. Her allegiance was to England and its allies.

"I see a worried look on your face," observed Walter.

"Because I am worried. I worry about where this conversation is going. I know where I don't want it to go."

Walter tried to interrupt, but she wouldn't let him. "No. Let me finish what I was going to say. I want you to know exactly who I am. Then you can speak."

He shrugged.

Sandra went back to her story. "It was in Bucharest as a teenager that I, by now a well-schooled Sandra, met Bill Stephenson, who, along with his wife, Mary, quickly saw some potential in me. Very soon with the assistance of the Stephensons I established myself as a very dear friend of influential people, both on the German as well as the British side." Sandra smiled as she said, "I was a witty, happy companion who could help the most stressed diplomat to unwind and enjoy life. By faking my legal records the Stephensons also saw to it that I entered the upper social class in Britain. For a person as young as I was, this life was exciting, as well as profitable for the Stephensons. I learned how to extract much important and sometimes secret information from my amiable friends."

"And what about Max, your father?" asked Walter. "What happened to him?"

"His last words of advice to me before I moved to London were that I should never let anyone see the real Sasha.

According to him, the only real safety in a world that the Nazis were beginning to dominate rested in conjecture and in contradictions. 'Never let anyone into your heart,' he advised. 'Never tell them who you really are.' I must, he said, 'always put love aside and choose friends and lovers from those who will always help you.' Max died shortly after I moved permanently to London."

Walter had wrapped his arms around her while she talked about her past. She found his warmth very comforting. "I will always protect you, my dear, just as Max would want," he told her.

She turned away. "I want to believe you. But you are a Nazi. How can I trust you?"

He turned her face to look at his. "I suppose it is because I am an important Nazi. I have built my own power base within the party. I shall always protect that base. For me to try to undermine the Nazi cause now would result in my death. But I am a Nazi only because the party will one day be the most important power in the world. However there is a caveat. That will not happen if Hitler bites off more than he can chew. Believe me, if we start a war which the United States enters, we will lose. It may take several years, but Germany will lose."

He moved to his real interest. "You say that Stephenson wants you to take someone or something in the Krakow area of Poland back to London?" he asked.

"I think so, but I'm not sure if that is right. I've done similar things before for Bill because he knows how well I know that area."

"So it could be something important that is being taken back to London that can't go through the normal channels. Right?"

"Possibly. But I can't talk about something when I don't have any information about it," she said cautiously. She had helped Stephenson many times to illegally bring items across borders, but she wouldn't mention that to Walter, either.

"I need your help, Sandra. If you love me, you will help me."

She looked at him sadly. "I will always help you. But not in ways that would make me a traitor."

"Think, Sandra," he said. "Do you have any idea of what it is that is being taken out of Poland? It's important. Let me tell you why. But how about a cup of coffee first?" He went to the flat's kitchen and brewed several cups.

"Horrible tasting, but it'll do," she said.

After they were comfortable, he picked up where he had left off a few minutes ago. "Find out for me what is soon to happen in Krakow, Poland next week. Please help me."

What should she say now? The truth was more than apparent that he was only interested in information. But to turn him down now might ruin Bill Stephenson's plans, whatever they were. This might not be the right time to make Walter angry. Of course she didn't believe him that he loved her, and for that she was sad. The truth was that she wanted Walter in her life. Just not as a Nazi.

"I will try to find out what I can about whether something important is happening in the Krakow area. I will tell you as soon as I know something," she said dully.

He lifted her high into the air and swung her around. "Here's to our happiness, my darling."

"I see Max in your eyes," Sandra said through her tears. "But I don't see him in your heart."

He wasn't certain what she meant, but it didn't matter.

"How will we communicate in Poland?" she asked.

They shared their Poland time schedules, arranging that she would meet him on a certain day and time at the Krakow Amadeus where she would be staying.

"I have to get back to the office now," he said. He turned to her. "Thank you, my love."

She couldn't help reaching out to touch him. "Feel how much I care for you."

"And I for you.'"

But she lied. All she felt was an excitement at the danger Walter represented. His danger excited her. She wondered if that was also the quality about her that excited him.

♦

Later when she was back at her flat she relived the time she had just spent with Walter.

She had to act. And it was an important decision that she must make. She wished that Max were beside her as he had been at many points in her life She had always valued and followed his advice. Just what would he say about Walter? She decided that she certainly could anticipate some of that because of the way that Max had carefully schooled her in his process of decision making.

She could still hear him telling her over and over to the point of boredom that there were certain behaviors that all of us must adhere to in our lives. She could hear the emphatic "must" that Max always used as he advised her. The first thing he would say, she was certain, was "save yourself by never acting compulsively." Next, he would probably say that "all that you do in life should be aimed at making yourself happy." Nothing works unless one is happy, he always believed. His final words she was sure would be that she must "do as little as possible to hurt anyone and as much as possible to help others." And above all else, "take advice only from those you can trust."

"But what if you aren't here?" she had asked.

Max had stared at her for a second before saying, "If I'm not around, call Uncle Androz." Uncle Androz and Max had been best friends for most of their lives, each a fighter against the ravages of war. And finally, "If the two of us aren't around, you are on your own. Act as you believe I would want you to act."

She remembered how Max had shaken his finger at her to emphasize each bit of advice as he spoke.

Today she came to a quick decision. It was time for her to start following Max's advice.

She walked to a nearby bookcase and reached her hand around to the back of the second shelf from the top for the key which she carried with her out of the flat. That key opened the door to the flat across from hers. Bill Stephenson owned this building and kept the flat across from hers for any emergencies she might have. No one knew about it but her. She picked up the phone that sat on the desk to dial a number on a completely secure line that could never be tapped nor could calls be traced.

Luck was on her side. "Uncle Androz!" she exclaimed gratefully. Quickly she explained all that had been said when she met Walter. "Help me to do the right thing," she asked.

He would. That he promised. It just so happened, he told her, that she would see him on her flight to Poland this Sunday. They would have time to talk then.

She remembered something else to tell him. "I have a feeling that Walter is hiding the fact that he has one or more Jewish ancestors. Could you verify that? It might be helpful for you to know that although Walter was born in Saarbrucken, Germany, he was raised in Luxembourg," she said.

Of course, he would check it out. "And immediately," he told her.

♦

When he hung up the phone after the call from Sandra, de Wiart, also known by Sandra as Uncle Androz, sat still for a few minutes, thinking about Walter's curiosity as to what was happening in Krakow. That was good. Slowly but surely they would ensnareWalter in a plot designed to make him look like a failure to his Nazi leaders.

De Wiart dialed another number and planted more information in Krakow about the death of the mysterious man in Bielany, a quiet suburb of Krakow. He made provisions for it to reach the ears of someone in Krakow who would send it to Walter immediately. He was certain that as soon as Walter got that information he'd dash off to that little cabin in the Polish woods. De Wiart chuckled. Walter would find nothing of value there. This was just one of the steps being taken to destroy him.

With his tall stature and his black eye patch and empty sleeve, de Wiart resembled an elegant pirate, according to the grateful Poles who loved him. Perhaps he did, de Wiart thought. If so, it was the Nazis whom he wished to capture. Unfortunately, that could not happen because the rest of the world would not help fight the Nazis. He knew that within a short while it was inevitable that Poland would fall to the Germans. But before it did, de Wiart would show the world the intelligence and bravery of the Poles. He would show the Germans up for the stupidity of their views. As well as the monsters that they were. He would send a message to the blind Germans who supported that idiot Hitler announcing to them that they were blinder than he was. What was going to happen to Walter Schellenberg because of Sandra would help prove that.

Sandra awoke the next morning with a sudden urge to call Walter. She wanted to hear his voice. Feelings don't die just because we will them to go away, she thought in defense. She was aware that it would take her heart quite a while to rid itself of Walter. But that didn't mean that she wouldn't do it.

Once more Sandra went to the safe apartment next door and called the temporary number which Walter had given her.

"*Brigadefuhrer* Schellenberg is out of town," a male voice told her. "Is this Miss Hoover? The *Brigadefuhrer* said he will meet you at the regular---"

"No," she said and hung up quickly. She felt herself blush. How blind had she been to think that he had been faithful to her. How stupid she had been to think that it would take a while before Walter was out of her system. It wouldn't be long at all. She must trust Uncle Androz to make her happy.

The assignment in Poland would begin soon. It couldn't start soon enough for her.

Chapter 7

It was time for Paul to meet with Bill Stephenson, a meeting that was long overdue, as far as Paul was concerned.

Something about this meeting was bothering him. Paul wasn't certain what it was, but he intended to find out before he accepted the assignment. He was a professional, and certainly information about assignments had been withheld from him in the past, just as was being done now. That was part of the game and Paul accepted it. But there was a distinct smell about this assignment which he didn't like. However, Dalton had eased some of Paul's inner doubts at their meeting by telling him that Stephenson would tell him more when they met to discuss what Dalton called the English "political scene."

Paul hoped that he would learn more. And as for that "political scene," Paul thought it was awful.

Then there was Stephenson to consider.

Paul hadn't been terribly impressed by the man at the von Ribbentrop reception. It wasn't his appearance, mind you, for he had learned that appearances are never accurate guides. It was Stephenson's apparent lack of self confidence. He might be one of the world's wealthiest men, but he certainly didn't give the appearance of someone who could deal with dissimulation and treachery, otherwise known as government intelligence agencies. In fact, Paul thought that the man seemed uncomfortable with the power that had been given him. Another thing Paul had noted was Stephenson's rather chummy relationship with the lovely violet-eyed Sandra Martin at the von Ribbentrop reception. They seemed too chummy, if one took into consideration the speed with which the limousine belonging to Nazi Walter Schellenberg had sped with her aboard to a rendezvous god knows where and about god knows what.

Paul clutched the file of information which Harry and David had compiled for him as he left to meet Hugh Dalton. The information Harry and Dave gave him about Sandra was incendiary. He looked forward to hearing Stephenson's attempt to explain it. As for Stephenson, the man, both Harry and David insisted that the man was brilliant as well as trustworthy. If anyone could clean up the rotten mess that English intelligence had become it would be Bill Stephenson, the two men emphasized. At least this proved to Paul that Churchill hadn't been drunk when he appointed Stephenson to direct government intelligence.

♦

"Hello, Paul." The limousine quickly pulled away from the curb when Hugh Dalton gave the chauffeur a signal. "You will meet Bill at a safe location outside London," explained Dalton.

"Right," Paul said.

They were quiet for most of the rest of the trip.

"Second floor." Dalton pointed to the correct building when they arrived at their destination. "Some one will meet you and take you to Stephenson's office."

Dalton spoke before Paul left. "Glad you are with us, Paul. We need you."

How does one answer that? "I'll do the best I can," Paul said cautiously.

♦

Although he tried not to show it, Bill Stephenson dreaded this meeting.

For one thing, Bill knew that Paul Duke, a professional in intelligence if there ever was one, must realize how little he was being told by Dalton and now him. Not that this was always possible, but a sparsity of information might be taken as an indication of the inept leadership of current English governmental intelligence agencies. Bill would try but it might not be possible to convince Paul that everything was under control. After all, look at the bungles which Military Intelligence had made recently But he'd try to win Paul's support. Bill sighed. They needed Paul.

When he arrived Paul was ushered into a smallish room filled with a long table that seated at least ten but held only one figure at the present time. Bill Stephenson sat at the far end of the table.

That jaw of Stephenson's was certainly a determined jaw. As for his face, his slightly drawn light eyebrows gave an intensity to it, although it was a face which one would have difficulty in describing, for there was no one overshadowing feature that drew attention, other than the jut of that jaw.

At the von Ribbentrop reception Paul had observed that Stephenson talked well, with a fluency which showed he probably always examined in advance all aspects of issues presented to him. He also smiled a great deal in public, as if he believed that a pleasant facade was always necessary. Perhaps that was a good thing, Paul decided, for when Stephenson was silent his mouth looked firm, even tight lipped and slightly nasty. Paul glanced at the man's well-cut features and his well-brushed fair hair. Very short in stature, Stephenson allowed himself to seem overwhelmed by the large furniture in the room. That might be just an act, Paul thought, for all in all, Paul would conclude from his appearance that Stephenson was a very direct, a very controlled, and a very focused man who was never overwhelmed by anything.

Stephenson glanced at Paul, smiled, and then looked quizzically at the empty table. He suggested that they sit closer to each other.

"We can talk about what you and I are about to undertake. I'm glad it's just the two of us. By the way, I'm Bill. Let's make this a productive meeting. No interruptions from others." His arm swept around the empty table. "I am going to be honest with you and I expect the same from you. The truth is that I need you. I'm trying to help Churchill keep Great Britain together. I can do it with your help. Let's begin by facing facts. I'm certain that you have heard about the chaotic situation at SIS." He shuffled a few papers in front of him as a way of looking down when he spoke about a matter that was obviously a great embarrassment to him.

Paul interrupted. "Before we go any further, Hugh Dalton gave me permission to have Harry Paine and David Christie work with me on this assignment. Is this acceptable to you? I have not told them what this is because I don't know myself."

"Fine," said Stephenson. "Those two have the highest clearance. I anticipated that you would want to work with them. Now back to the mess that we have to fix. I'm sure that you know about the capture of the two SIS agents and the information about our system which the Nazis now have."

Paul nodded. "The Venlo Incident."

"Walter Schellenberg was responsible for that. You have met him, haven't you?"

Paul said that he had.

"Incidentally, did you also know that he sent us a note about what he did?"

No. Paul hadn't heard about that.

Stephenson reached into a drawer and pulled out a sheet which he handed to Paul without any comment.

Dear English SIS administrators:

We wish to thank you for the wonderful opportunity which you gave us to illustrate to the entire world what complete asses all of you are.

Actually, it was quite easy to accomplish this task. Can you possibly put on your thinking caps and plan some activities that stretch the German brain? Otherwise, competing against you will be too boring to even contemplate.

Your friends in German Intelligence

Stephenson's face flushed. "Schellenberg will pay for that, I assure you. Now back to our subject. When war starts and Churchill is prime minister he intends to appoint you to head up our communication facilities. We are presently working to plan a system for you. You may be based in Switzerland, an ideal spot because of the country's neutrality. That will be down the road a bit. Let's talk about your present assignment. You still have a fluency in Polish, don't you? We have a mission in Poland that must be undertaken within the next few days at the latest."

Paul nodded. "As soon as possible, I would say." He wondered how many more days Poland had before the Nazis invaded the country.

Bill said, "I'm assigning Sandra Martin to go to Poland with you. Take Harry and David as well."

Paul could feel his lips tighten.

"What's wrong, Paul?"

"Am I to speak freely?" Paul wanted this meeting to start off with some honesty from both of them.

"Absolutely."

"Attending the von Rippentrop reception was an eye opener for me. I felt as if I were surrounded by a country of Hitler appeasers."

"You are."

"But I was also concerned by some other things and people I saw other than appeasers. Namely Sandra Martin. I'm almost certain that she is working in intelligence for you. However, she generates an inordinate amount of interest from the public, primarily I think as a sex symbol. I watched her behavior with Ambassador von Schulenburg at the reception long enough to say that I'm certain that Martin uses him as a source of information for us. However, her blatant behavior with him must compromise him in the eyes of the Nazis. And that very important Nazi, Walter Schellenberg, was there at the reception, carefully watching her behavior."

Paul was quiet for a little while before he spoke again. "And then there's the fact that she is a Jew."

Stephenson's voice was just as quiet. "How did you find that out? We've done our best to keep it hidden. Because of England's strict Alien laws."

"Thank Harry and David for that. They knew Sandra's mother was living in London when she married and so they checked the records of every synagogue in London."

"That was good work," said Stephenson.

"Sandra may be a great intelligence agent. But one day that is not going to matter. What it does mean is that Sandra is an ideal target for a blackmailer. Come the war Great Britain is going to be hard on illegal aliens like her, let alone illegal aliens who hold responsible jobs in English intelligence. At that point she will be of no use to you."

"Let me dispel some of your doubts about her, Paul. It's true, I've used her and successfully, too, for several years—

first in Bucharest and then here in London. She's good with men when she plays a silly flirt. That is the role we gave her. But she's far from that."

Paul countered that argument quickly. "But what about her behavior with von Schulenburg? If you were Schellenberg, how would you react to seeing how easily a silly flirt can compromise a German Ambassador?" Paul left the question floating in the air.

Stephenson looked down at his hands when Paul finished. "You will direct this assignment, Paul. In that function you will also supervise Sandra. All I can add is that you are the only one so far who has seen through her cover."

"But Germans like Canaris and Schellenberg are just as bright as I am—or more."

"It's your decision to make about Sandra," said Bill. "You have the power to drop her from our program at any time after the trip to Poland. All I ask is that for this mission to Poland you follow the plans that we have already made. These include Sandra. You must trust me that her presence is vital for this assignment. Can you accept this, Paul?"

Paul nodded, reluctantly, but he nodded.

Bill looked carefully at Paul. "It's time for me to tell you more about your assignment in Poland."

Paul sat back, eager to hear what Bill was at last going to share with him. Bill said, "I'm nothing but a pencil pusher and a numbers cruncher who tries to make everything work efficiently. But I'm not a hero. You are, and so is the man directing this assignment." He paused. "I'm talking about Androz de Wiart, probably one of the most loved and revered man in Poland."

Bill's words caused Paul to catch his breath. He knew that de Wiart was more than that. De Wiart was almost a religious icon for the Poles as well as for his native Brits. Widely believed to be an illegitimate son of the Belgian King Leopold, de Wiart had established his reputation in World War I by outstanding bravery. in spite of his horrendous injuries.

Bill continued. "De Wiart spent the interwar years on a large 500,000-acre estate in eastern Poland as the guest of the Polish Prince Karol Radziwill in gratitude for his efforts for the Polish. In July 1939 he was recalled and appointed to his old job as head of the British Military Mission for Poland. This is the position he now holds. Let me start at the beginning. Churchill, de Wiart, and I believe that the Nazis will invade Poland within the month. Since England and its allies refuse to arm Poland, Poland will probably fall very quickly. At the present time, any Pole with a brain is getting anything of value out of Poland. And that includes Polish plans for weapons or materials or military secrets that the Nazis will grab as soon as they invade. And this is where you enter the equation, Paul."

Paul nodded, eager to hear more details.

"According to de Wiart there are Nazi spies in Poland right now attempting to identify and keep anything of value from leaving Poland until the Nazis come to power. And speaking about 'anything of value,' de Wiart says that by next week Polish scientists in the northern part of Poland will attempt to smuggle a tremendously important military secret out of Poland to England. For many months Polish scientists have begged English officials for help in getting the material out of the country. But the British refused. I cannot understand that position, but that is what we face. Now, because it is late and because the Germans are looking for just such attempts, it is iffy as to whether any smuggling operation will or will not work. But the Poles intend to make a last ditch effort to smuggle the materials out of Poland and to give them to the British to use during the war that is almost here. According to de Wiart, it is no exaggeration to say that what is to be smuggled is so important that its ownership may make the difference between who wins or loses the next war."

The two men sat silently, each thinking of the implications of what Bill had just said.

"However, de Wiart has an idea, a scheme to fool the Nazis and keep them from stealing this powerful Polish military secret." Bill looked directly at Paul. "This is where de Wiart needs you. You and he are going to camouflage the smuggling attempt next week from Warsaw with a carefully orchestrated campaign at the same time that will throw the Germans off the track. It will be your responsibility to convince them that yes, a smuggling attempt is going to take place, but the smuggling will take place in Krakow and that it is of jet propulsion plans developed by Polish scientists."

Paul sat up in excitement. "That's clever, but a difficult strategy to pull off. Every piece in it has to fit or the Germans will get suspicious."

"You're right," said Bill. "Precisely why we want you to head up the operation. De Wiart plans to make it work. According to him, the key to something like this is to have elements of truth sprinkled throughout the plan. The story he has concocted is that for years de Wiart has been subsidizing research into jet propulsion by a scientist friend of his in the Krakow area. Last week his friend had a heart attack and it was de Wiart who rushed his friend to a local hospital. However, it was too late. His friend died. It is that fictitious death that de Wiart plans to weave into a story that will trick the Nazis. The Nazis will learn through rumors that a representative of the dead man's family will arrive from Canada to settle the estate. Rumors will also be spread that these important military plans are lying around somewhere in Krakow, waiting to be found by anyone. The story will also be spread that the supposed cousin of the dead scientist is in reality an English spy looking for the missing plans. According to de Wiart that rumor is already generating an influx of German Nazis to the area. One of those Germans starting to sniff around the area is the man I want to trap. Walter Schellenberg wants those plans so that he can impress Hitler with his ability. And I want Walter Schellenberg."

Bill stopped to take a long drink from the water carafe on the table. He said, "We want you and your group to become the family of the dead man and then lead the Nazis on a long goose chase that allows the other smuggling in the north of Poland to be carried out without any difficulties. At this point I think that we need to throw some credit Sandra's way for her part in directing Schellenberg's attention to Krakow."

"If that is what she has done, you are right," Paul said very sincerely. "Sandra deserves credit for what she has been doing."

"But your response to her was correct, Paul, given the circumstances." Bill added, "It was just that you didn't know everything. If I had been you I would have been very suspicious if my boss kept insisting that I employ someone whose behavior was inappropriate. One of the pieces that you didn't know is that de Wiart has been the best friend of Sandra's family for over 20 years. To Sandra, de Wiart is Uncle Androz. Her actions were taken at his request."

"I'm sorry that I didn't know that. I didn't give her a chance."

"I couldn't tell you before, and I apologize for that. But let's get back to our plan. Do you see what I am saying? You must play a role if we are to pull a fast one on the Nazis. We must pretend that you have or are guarding some secret with your life. You must make Schellenberg salivate at the thought of his capturing such a prize."

Bill got quiet. "There's another part to this. The Poles are in for a rough time when the Nazi troops arrive. I have already been told that Nazi plans have been drawn up to make Poland the center for concentration camps, which is a fancy term for extermination camps. It will be up to the few men like de Wiart to inspire and keep the Poles fighting for their country against tremendous odds. De Wiart believes that it time for him to speak to the Polish nation and ready them for what will be coming."

"He's right," said Paul. "If anyone can, de Wiart can inspire them with enough strength and courage to get through all of this."

"That is why I am asking you to also take on the job of protecting de Wiart next week in Poland when he attends the religious ceremonies at Jasna Gora and then makes a speech to the more than 50,000 pilgrims expected to be there."

Paul nodded. "Jasna Gora is the right place for de Wiart to make such an important address. Have you ever visited Jasna Gora, Bill?"

"No. I wish that I had. But that's where you are going, Paul. What do you know about it?"

"I visited Czestochowa about ten years ago and have always had a longing to return to see more of it. There is so much to see that no one visit is sufficient. You know that the Monastery there, Jasna Gora, is one of the top three Catholic shrines in the world?"

Bill nodded.

"It is the country's greatest place of pilgrimage—for most Poles it is the country's spiritual capital. The monastery was founded in 1382 by Pauline monks who came from Hungary. The image of the Black Madonna of Czestochowa, a painting to which miraculous powers are attributed, is Jasna Gora's most precious treasure. The painting depicting the Virgin with the Christ Child, was probably painted in 1434 on top of an older Byzantine icon, the original Black Madonna, which was damaged by robbers in 1430. However, the scars of the damages were left on the cheek of the Madonna. The Monastery has survived several sieges, including a legendary 40-day siege by the Swedes in 1655. It is the perfect place for de Wiart to address the Poles, Bill."

"But will you be able to protect him on this pilgrimage?" asked Bill.

Paul could understand Bill's concerns for de Wiart's safety.

"Of course I can do it." he said. "But I will need many men," he added.

"De Wiart can call on his faithful Poles for security," Bill said.

"Does De Wiart have any time for me to meet with him before the trip so that we can coordinate activities?" asked Paul.

Bill nodded. "You will meet with de Wiart this weekend at my home. You can arrange everything at that time. Here are some more details of our plan. We want you, and of course, Harry and David, to travel together to Krakow. Sandra will be traveling there by herself. Your cover name is Charles Scott Devereau of Montreal, just as it was at the von Ribbentrop reception."

Paul nodded.

"The story we've expanded on is that your late cousin Tad Babij's 's son, Jan, of Krakow, has died and left you everything in his will. Jan lived in a home rented from Tomas and Sofia Janusek in Bielany, a suburb of Krakow. The Januseks sent you a telegram about Jan's death and you have already responded to it and told them when you will arrive at the local Krakow airport. They will meet you there and take you to their home. But before they do, they must identify themselves by holding up a card at the airport which will list your name. The Januseks will arrange for Jan's quick cremation before you arrive, citing as their reason his instructions in his will. They will also arrange for a memorial service for Jan at a local church. In addition they will also take you to the local lawyer who will make arrangements to probate Jan's will, as well as make any arrangements to have his property placed in your hands. All the money proceeds will be sent to your Canadian address. Trust the Januseks to tell you what else you must do. But there is another important part to this."

He paused for emphasis.

"Two days after your arrival in Krakow, Sandra will arrive in Bielany. All of you will travel together to Jasna Gora Monastery in Czestochowa. While there you will pick up a copy of the famous Black Madonna painting which your dead cousin ordered. As identification you will say that you intend to take it home to England as a memento of Jan. The next day Sandra will lead you to a private airfield outside Czestochowa and you will all be flown home. Make sure that you have the painting. It is another of our red herrings. We are trying to suggest to the Nazis that some secret military information may be hidden somewhere in the picture, although you and I both know that is not correct. Don't ever let the print out of your sight for a second, because we hope that it will be an important part of our smokescreen to confuse the Nazis and leave them false clues everywhere in the Krakow area.. If you were a German spy, wouldn't you want to consider that the package might contain the jet propulsion plans?"

They sat there for a minute in silence, as if the information which they had shared with each other should be absorbed in silence. Paul wondered what was really being smuggled out of Poland. He decided that it looked as if he would not find out today.

"This is enough for today," Bill said. "Think about any questions you might have. I'd like all of you to meet with me at my home tomorrow. Is that all right?" He looked into Paul's eyes. "You are one of only four people who know something important will be smuggled out of Poland. Churchill, de Wiart, you, and me. No one else is to know. It is a tremendous responsibility that the four of us hold. I think that you well understand." They shook hands after making arrangements about tomorrow's visit.

Stephenson returned to his office a few minutes later after seeing Paul to Dalton's limousine for Paul's return to London.

A side door opened and Winston Churchill entered. "Did Paul accept the assignment?"

"Yes."

"It has to work, Bill. We need some good luck."

"Paul is one of those perfectionists who will do exactly what is asked of him. We've planned everything carefully. Nothing can go wrong."

Churchlll winced. "I've heard that before. I even said that about the Dardanelles in World War I. The English public has never forgiven me for that."

"Trust me."

"De Wiart will meet with the group at your house?" asked Churchill.

"Of course."

Churchill puffed on his cigar. "De Wiart and Paul will make it all work."

Chapter 8

"Your chariot awaits."

Paul was surprised to see Sandra, and not Stephenson's chauffeur, when the bell rang at his flat early the next morning and her perpetually smiling face appeared.

"What a difference in your appearance from the von Ribbentrop reception," she exclaimed. "But you do dowdy very well, I must say. You might start a new trend for poorly fitting clothes."

He laughed at that and did a half bow. Bill Stephenson had probably told her all about his intent to be anonymous.

"I'm ready," he announced to her, hastily shoving his arms into his jacket. The truth was that he hadn't planned to invite her in; in fact, he had intended to give her as little opportunity as possible to learn more about him. After that thought, though, he decided that it might be time to reassess his behavior and his thoughts. He wasn't proud of them. Why was it that he was so negative about her? After all, her connection to de Wiart should help him to see her with new eyes. And to be honest, there was something very appealing about her, even though he couldn't quite put his finger on it. It is sex, an voice inside him wanted to shout, but he silenced it.

All of that should have lessened his distrust of her, but it didn't. Was all this mere jealousy on his part, he wondered. He hoped that he was beyond that. The plain truth was simple. De

Wiart notwithstanding, nothing so far had convinced him that he could trust Sandra.

"Let's go," he said with a smile. "My clothes fit today, so you won't be ashamed to be with me."

Soon the limousine was whisking them out of the city and westward to an area increasingly short on suburbs and strong on farmland. On the relatively quick trip he and Sandra talked little at first. However, he decided it might be expedient to start again and see if he might begin a dialogue with her. He asked questions about the Stephensons and heard a very positive message. They were "wonderful," according to her. Whatever that means, he thought. Paul soon decided that Sandra was one of those people whose sentences always end in exclamation marks.

However, he did obtain a complete response from her when he asked about the Stephenson home.

He learned, for example, that Bill Stephenson was paying all the bills to rent a site from which various intelligence programs would operate during the next war. Alnwyk Castle, where they were going today, was that site, she said. "Not only will all the planning and training for the SOE program emanate at Alnwyk, but it will also be the center for other intelligence programs. You know what the Special Operations Executive Program is, don't you? I direct a part of that program."

He nodded. The SOE was a very complex organization which in wartime would plan and execute programs of dropping spies into occupied countries for infiltration and destruction purposes. Stephenson had told him that the SOE would be Sandra's major activity. Paul was skeptical of using Sandra in such work. SOE work required highly trained directors if it were to work. And the mortality rate for spies in the program was very high. It might be splendid to give one's life for one's country but he himself would rather join a program where the odds were better than those in the SOE.

Relax, Paul, he told himself. Give her a chance.

Sandra went on talking, nonstop. "Ultimately a part of the castle will serve as an army hospital when casualties start. Bill is paying a huge sum for the upkeep and maintenance of the old castle."

"Alnwyk Castle?" Paul was impressed. "That's a major English historical landmark," he said. "It's one of England's most beautiful castles. Every Englishman knows that famous name."

Rapidly their limousine moved closer to their destination, which Paul knew was near the village of Newberry and on the border between Berkshire and Hampshire.

The closer they got the more excited Paul became. "I remember touring the castle when I was about eight," he said. "I came from a family of farmers and I had never seen anything like Alnwyk. I remember asking my mother if we had suddenly gone to Heaven."

Soon the limousine rounded the side of a mountain and arrived at a towering spot from which one could see Alnwyk. The chauffeur stopped to give them time to absorb the view.

"I've been here many times this year, but I never get tired of this view," Sandra acknowledged.

Paul said nothing, but just stared down the path which ended in the sand-colored brick castle. Looking at Sandra he said, "I was smart for an eight-year old, wasn't I? This really *is* Heaven."

The rectangular Alnwyk sat in the center of its universe. From where he stood Paul saw that the castle occupied the top of a hill and dominated what he estimated to be more than 1,000 acres of sweeping parkland surrounding it.

Even the castle itself was immense. Paul stopped counting after he roughly estimated that there must be at least 100 rooms fronting each of the four sides of the castle. In addition, seven imposing spires rose from the castle, each of which Paul believed to hold at least twenty rooms.

Beyond the castle were stables, nurseries, formal paths, and immense follies. In the distance, the land beyond the buildings became flat, allowing him a view of various towns and villages far in the distance. The palate of colors changed from the deep green around the castle to the bluish haze of what existed far away.

And far away in time as well, he thought. Originally the estate of the Bishops of Winchester, the castle has been home to the same family since 1679, although it had been redesigned many times since then. Even the grounds of this majestic Victorian Gothic edifice bore witness to the brilliance of English landscape artists.

"Capability Brown designed these grounds, I believe," he said to Sandra in a questioning tone.

"He did," she said.

When they had seen enough they re-entered the limousine and silently and slowly approached Alnwyk, where Bill and Mary Stephenson stood outside the front doors waiting for them. After hugging Sandra and shaking Paul's hand, Stephenson introduced Paul to his smiling wife who had her arm around Sandra's waist.

"Unless I rented the Taj Mahal I could never make a better impression than pretending to be the master of Alnwyk, could I? Isn't this the most beautiful place in the world?" asked Stephenson.

"It's heaven," Paul said with a straight face. He recounted to the Stephensons his introduction to Alnwyk as a young boy.

Once their luggage was carried into the reception area, Stephenson turned to them ruefully. "I'm so sorry to have to change our plans for today, but I have no choice. I only recently learned from Churchill that William Donovan will arrive here in 45 minutes."

This last statement was a bombshell to everyone. Everyone there understood the importance of William Donovan to England's future survival. "Wild Bill," as he was called in America, definitely had President Roosevelt's ear.

Just recently, President Roosevelt had decided to send his chief intelligence consultant, multimillionaire Wall Street lawyer William J. Donovan, to England on a secret mission. He was charged by Roosevelt with gauging Britain's ability to withstand German aggression when and if Germany marched into Poland. From Donovan's report FDR would decide whether or not to secretly provide the English with supplies and money. That would happen only if Donovan approved of the English efforts to prepare for war, for without the support of the U.S. there was little hope for British success.

In deliberating about his decision, Donovan had made his first trip to England three weeks ago. On that trip he spoke with Bill Stephenson at length about overall plans, and then at Bill's suggestion that Sandra be his guide, Donovan had personally visited and approved key English sites in the war effort as well as specific departments which Stephenson had set into operation.

That first visit by Donovan had been made in an old 1924 two-seater car, the only vehicle available in the car pool that day when Sandra chauffeured Donovan through the English countryside on his first secret mission to evaluate England's preparations for war.

Prior to their ride, Sandra had been told by Stephenson that she would be responsible for winning Donovan's support. The political scene in London, with the SIS chief terribly unfavorable to the SOE and wishing to close it down, underscored the importance of Sandra's task. In disclosing and showing what the SOE and Stephenson were accomplishing, Sandra obviously swayed Donovan to write a favorable recommendation to Roosevelt when he returned to the United States from his first trip.

As Stephenson privately remarked later to Paul, it was obvious that some kind of "unspoken" understanding had developed, as Stephenson discreetly put it, between Sandra and Donovan on that first trip.

Sex is what that understanding is called, Paul thought to himself. It was interesting, he decided, how often he found himself using the word "sex"now that Sandra had joined their group. But then he realized that Sandra used more than just the word for sex.

As if reading Paul's mind, Stephenson said, "I don't care what it was. We won Roosevelt's tacit approval to support us. And we got the money."

Bill apologized for having to rearrange today's activities. "I'm sorry, Paul. I have no choice. My idea is that you, Donovan, and I will meet briefly after Donovan arrives. I understand that Donovan must leave tomorrow. We'll also schedule a longer meeting between the three of us later after your return from Poland. As for today, Sandra will again guide Donovan to the new sites and people that he didn't see on his last visit."

Stephenson enumerated exactly what he wanted Sandra to cover today with Donovan. "Is that clear?" He looked at her intently, knowing that only Sandra had the expertise to give Donovan an overview of SOE's rapid but seemingly chaotic growth. She alone would be able to show him how SOE's scope had been widened and how the average Brit, not the upper class appeasers, would fight for his or her country.

"Don't try to hide the fact to Donovan that there are many appeasers in this country," Bill advised her. "He will know that you are lying. Just show him how everyone is working to be ready for war when it comes." Stephenson added one last task for her. It would also be her responsibility to get Donovan to his plane tomorrow.

"I have no objections to that, sir," she said. She turned to Paul. "Sorry for the postponement. I will be here tomorrow early for our meeting," she promised. "Have Mary save one of cook's good biscuits for me."

Donovan arrived soon after.

After Bill did his introductions, Donovan reached out for Paul's arm. "It is indeed a pleasure, sir," Donovan said, "to be in your company. Your career has been a lifelong service to your country. When King George V knighted you in his words as among the 'greatest of all soldiers,' and a 'moral symbol' who handles well the 'sometimes tawdriness of human behavior,' you became the only Englishman ever knighted based entirely for your exploits in espionage. I look forward to working with you in the future."

Donovan was obviously glad to have the opportunity to meet Paul, the man who ultimately would be second in command to Bill Stephenson once English intelligence was overhauled and ready for the war.

After a few minutes of conversation, the Stephensons led the group from the drawing room into Alnwyk's elaborate dining room for a formal lunch. Before Sandra and Donovan left, Donovan looked so obviously impressed that Mary Stephenson on the spot improvised a very quick look at some of the magnificent rooms in the castle. The library and the saloon were everyone's favorites. More than anyone else, Paul admired the beauty of the entire house. These were rooms that were meant to return to, rooms that soothed and brought peace to the soul. Alnwyk might be a romantic dream of an England which had long since vanished, but it was also a reminder of a gentler world that could be created if everyone joined in to help.

"This is what we are fighting for," Mary said quietly to Donovan after the brief tour ended.

Donovan nodded.

"I'll be your guide for the entire castle the next time you are here," Mary promised Donovan. "Now it's time for you two to get started," Bill said. Looking at Donovan he said, "This time you will have a car that is in better condition. Now that's an improvement, isn't it?"

Sandra decided that she would start Donovan's visit today by letting him talk to the people who were helping to establish channels of English intelligence once more. She drove him back to London so that he might speak to people who were involved in the effort.

"No one knows why you are here," she warned Donovan. "Let's keep it that way." She showed him actual training classes currently in operation.

Next she stopped off at Hyde Park in London in order to allow Donovan to watch a rally of Blackshirts led by Sir Oswald Mosley and his British Union of Fascists. Mosley was the husband of Diana Mitford, of the prominent Mitford family and the sister of Unity Mitford, one of the supposed mistresses of Hitler. "We allow even the enemies of democracy to spout their treason," Sandra explained to Donovan. "That's one of the things democracies must allow."

The Blackshirt Rally turned nasty and soon the two found themselves listening to anti-Jewish verbal filth that seemed to come straight from the mouth of the Fuhrer.

"We are fighting all of this," Sandra told Donovan. "We have little money to pay our side. However, everyone who understands what a crossroads England is at is donating his time. We need your help, Bill."

Following this, she called ahead to some offices to alert people that she would be stopping by with a guest.

Colin McVean "Gubby" Gubbins was Donovan's first interviewee. A descendant of a captain of dragoons who campaigned for Oliver Cromwell in Ireland in the 1600's, Gubby had become a specialist in guerrilla warfare. It was Gubby's present task to train future soldiers in air defense, since everyone understood that one day the Germans would bomb England. "But I'm doing my best to train whoever I can and to spread the word that we need money."

Maurice Buckmaster, Sandra's boss at SOE's Section F, the section that trained and then had parachusted agents into occupied countries, was in his office when Donovan and Sandra came by. Cautious and often plodding in his actions, Buckmaster was building an organization that would, hopefully, make few mistakes. In Buckmaster's office Donovan also had the opportunity to meet Indian Princess Noor Inayat Khan, one of the brave recruits in training to be dropped by air as spies.

After the day of inspection was completed, Donovan and Sandra stopped for a drink in the public bar of a roadhouse slightly out of London. He took a room for them overlooking a motorway that was congested with traffic.

From the room they shared they could see a silver gray London in the distance. The world stretched out before them was the one Sandra now called home, the vast conglomerate of urban living that she loved. The tall skyscrapers and the lights pleased fascinated her. She believed it to be a world to be respected and protected.

"London is the affirmation of what we believe in," she said.

He and Sandra reached for each other when Donovan closed the drapes.

Donovan's flight back was mid morning, which gave them time to be together before he left. On the trip to the airport she made a stop. After that she delivered him to an RAF flying boat at Plymouth Sound that set course for Gibraltar, Britain's first imperial coaling port and military bastion. With him Donovan carried the package she had ordered for him. It included a flask of hot turtle soup, a hamper of fresh lobster, cold pheasant, Stilton cheese, and three bottles of Moselle.

♦

Not many days after that, Roosevelt sent a cable to Churchill, thanking him for the "magnificent" welcome Donovan had received on his trip.

"Donovan was clearly on our side," Paul heard Sandra say.

I'm sure that Donovan was on your side, Sandra, as well as on every part of your body, Paul thought when Sandra told him enthusiastically about Donovan's successful trip. *How snide I am,* Paul decided. But accurate.

Chapter 9

True to her word, Sandra arrived at Alnwyk in time to join the group for brunch.

She arrived full of enthusiasm about her time yesterday with Donovan. "He seemed very impressed with what we are doing," she announced happily.

She was certain that he would be giving FDR a favorable impression. "And that means money for our programs," she said. Everyone was delighted to hear that. Sandra's ego seemed satisfied with the praise being heaped on her, thought Paul.

Calm down, Paul told himself. So what if the woman was looking for praise about her part in it? *The important thing is getting US money,* he told himself. Anyway, he wasn't jealous of what Sandra had achieved, he tried to convince himself. It was more about how she did it, he decided.

During a lull in the conversation at the dining table, Sandra turned impulsively to Paul, who was sitting next to her. "You and I have a lot to talk about. How about if I take you to see some of the things that we're doing in Intelligence? Sort of an abbreviated version of what I showed Donovan these last two days. I'll tell you what I showed him. You and I can talk while I drive."

She looked at Paul.

"That's fine with me," he said, noncommittally, although inside he was surprised to realize that he welcomed the opportunity to be alone with her before they left for Poland. He hoped that a conversation alone with her might straighten out some of his conflicted feelings about her.

Bill Stephenson also seemed pleased at her offer. "We won't expect you back here for dinner. When you return this evening we'll finalize your travel plans."

With that the two were off.

They were quiet until the last view of Alnwyk disappeared. After that it seemed easier to talk, even if they just spoke about the general plans and dates which Stephenson had made for their trip.

They both expected to get more specifics from Stephenson at their meeting tonight. Paul was beginning to feel more secure about this trip.

"You don't like me, do you?" She had said this very suddenly and without rancor, and with perhaps what sounded to him as a drop of sadness that it was true.

Because he hadn't expected it, he fumbled to find an appropriate answer. "I've learned not to like or dislike anyone I don't know," he said to deflect her question. "But I can be honest."

He waited for a response to that, determined to end the discussion if she got confrontational.

"What do you think of me?" she asked, facing him with a rather tremulous look that was attempting to be a smile.

He was certain of what he would like to say, but also certain that he couldn't say it. He decided to once again circle around the truth. "You are well aware of how beautiful you are. In fact, I wonder if you don't use that beauty in a public way."

He took a deep breath and plunged deeper. "Your behavior strikes me as adolescent, although that may be a *persona* which you adopt for the public. I don't know. However, we do need to know more about each other if we are to work together. I really want to know how you respond to events, particularly emergencies. I also want to know what drives you and whether you work well in a group as well as individually."

He took a quick look at her face to see her reaction to these words. She looked troubled. He said, "I expect that you want to know the same about me. Right?"

She didn't answer that, but instead said, "Let me pull into the next car park so that we can talk."

He didn't speak until after she parked. "Let's start off with the fact that I already know a lot about you, Sandra. And because of that I'm fearful of you. You seem to thrive on danger. That in itself is a dangerous trait for any intelligence officer. My philosophy in Intelligence has always been to avoid as much danger as I could. Often that isn't possible, but usually it is. But once I'm in danger, I play to win. As far as you are concerned, I don't intend to have my life affected by someone who seems to court adventure."

Abruptly she said, "What else do you know about me?"

"Not that much more." Evasiveness seemed a smart approach to him.

Sandra's reaction was surprising. Without a missed beat she launched into a lengthy monologue about her life from childhood up to yesterday.

Paul's mouth fell open as he learned everything there was to know about all the men in her life, starting with her father, family, friends, and even Germans, today, ranging from the devoted Schulenburg to the Nazi Walter Schellenberg.

To be honest, Paul had no idea of why she was doing this. *Enough! You've told me more than I want to know about you!* was what he wanted to tell her, but couldn't. She would be hurt. All he could do was place his arm around her shoulder and hope that she interpreted it as a gesture of concern from a friend. If Sandra decided one day to write her autobiography,

Paul decided that it would probably be more of a shocker than Fanny Hill's adventures.

"You've seen how successful I am with people?" she asked, obviously seeking his approval.

He shook his head. "That may be. But all I've seen is the way that you've made relationships very public." What else could be said to someone whose emotional background was so shaky? "All that I suggest is that you hold back your emotions. Keep the real Sandra hidden."

"That's a coincidence. That's exactly what Max used to tell me."

For a totally different reason, Paul was certain, although he said nothing. Instead, he reached out to hold her hand. "What are you going to show me today?"

"Wait a while."

After they drove a bit, Sandra spoke again. "This is the village of Winchelsea. Where I own a cottage. Come on," Sandra said. "I'm going to show you what I am fighting the Nazis to protect."

The weather is frequently black and windy in the villages that sit on the English Channel, but today there was one of those breaks in the weather that makes English days much more bearable. Huddled in heavy coats, Sandra and Paul tramped around the village that had been designed by French King Edward I in 1288 when he left his other domain in Aquitaine in France to create Winchelsea. It was developed on the gridiron principle of the French *bastides,* Sandra said. "The local government in Winchelsea is the only one of its kind left in England. It is called a *jurat* which is appointed by the mayor and parish church counselors after the fashion of medieval Norman France, which once ruled here."

She explained that Winchelsea is one of the ancient Cinque Port English villages that sit on the English Channel. "It's hard to believe but we are only minutes by air from Hamburg, Germany," she said. "This little village has confronted invaders since 1359, when the Brits sailed from Winchelsea to disperse the Spanish Armada. Now the townfolk here ignore upheavals across the Channel. They know that England can endure anything."

"Winchelsea ia the place I go to when I want to forget how bad the world is becoming," she said. She pointed to the village church ahead of them. St. Thomas a Becket Church, Winchelsea's seven-hundred year old church, was dedicated to the martyr of Canterbury who had been murdered by barons who mistook the wishes of their king.

"Many years ago, French marauders used to frequently pour ashore to butcher or rape the worshipers huddled in the church," she said. "I feel close to the average Englishman who through the years has always been forced to fight for freedom. Unlike the present archbishop of Canterbury who currently urges appeasement with Hitler," she said bitterly. "I wonder how St. Thomas a Becket would feel about that."

They sat for a while in her cottage. She sat quietly, her hands in her lap, obviously satisfied with the place she called home. "This suits me," she said. "My cottage always welcomes me."

After they spoke for a while, she took Paul's arm. "Let's go into the church and pray for God's help for England. I want you to know that I want it just as much as you do." They sat in one of the pews in the empty chapel and prayed, not for divine intervention, but for all sides to seek peace rather than death.

It was time to return to Alnwyk.

"Hurry to the car, Paul. The winds are picking up here on the coast."

"Thank you for today. I've learned a lot of good things about you," Paul said softly.

"I'm glad."

Soon they were on their way back to Alnwyk. When they were quite close to the castle Sandra suddenly bore left instead of right. Paul was surprised to see a small airplane hangar only a few miles from the castle.

"I've got an idea," she said.

Paul groaned, "You and your ideas. What is this one?"

"I'm going to take you up for a few minutes," she said.

He groaned again.

"Trust me."

"I never trust anyone who says that. Seriously, do you have a pilot's license?"

"Of course," she said. "Why would you even ask?"

Deftly she opened the hangar door with a key, and within a few minutes had taxied a small Gypsy Moth biplane out of the hangar. It was an old model, for it looked like its fabric wings were held together by outdated wooden struts and wires. But it appeared to have received excellent care and maintenance.

Sandra sat confidently at the controls in the rear cockpit, and when she pointed her finger at the open front cockpit. he climbed in. Slowly the plane climbed through layers of clouds before it broke out into dazzling blue skies.

"That was a great takeoff," he yelled. Right after that she circled a few times before making a very smooth landing.

They both got out of the plane. She grinned at him. "I looked good, didn't I? I'm still learning. Some day I'll be a competent pilot. You just wait."

"That was excellent, Sandra. Now get back into the plane. This time you get into the front cockpit."

She watched from her seat as Paul grabbed the control column and put his feet on the rudder pedals. His left hand was on the throttle and his right hand was on the rudder pedals.

"It's time for some loop the loop!" he shouted. The plane first dove and then pulled out into a steep climb. When they were upside down, he heard her excited screams of pleasure as they headed down again. Before he landed he took the planes through many spins and dives.

"I can't believe how good you are," she said when they had landed and she was able to catch her breath.

"Thank you, Madame. I fly whenever I can."

"I want a lesson from you."

"And you shall have it. As soon as we return from Poland."

"No. I want it now." She took his hand and pulled him into the hangar, leading him to a narrow cot along one wall.

"Here," she said. Her hand put his on her breast. "Teach me how to fly as well as you do." Her hands were taking off his clothes while her lips and fingers explored his body.

"Let's," she kept saying.

His trembling fingers wanted to join her in saying, "Let's" over and over again, but he couldn't.

"Do it," she whispered. "Now."

"I can't." He tried to find the words that would explain, but couldn't.

She saw how upset he was. "Don't be sad. I understand," she said.

"It's just--" His voice cracked. "I feel as if we are two strangers trying to convince ourselves that sex is the vehicle that will turn us into friends. It doesn't do that, you know." *What a stilted little speech I just gave,* Paul thought with embarrassment. *Unfortunately it is true,* he told himself.

"Just a few more moments together," she said. She ran her fingers through his hair. "I want you to know that I am a nickname person."

The sudden shift of the conversation utterly puzzled Paul.

She tried to explain. "It means that I give nicknames to all the people I like. Thus we share a secret. I have one for you. Would you like to hear it?"

"I suppose I would," he said hesitantly. "It all depends on whether you like me or not."

"I do. You are now PS, not Paul. At least, when we are alone. You are a big PS, a good addition to my life, I must say. Seriously though, I wonder what PS literally means? I think it is Latin, but I'm not certain."

"And I have a nickname for you," he said. "I bet you can't guess what GG stands for, can you?"

"Not a clue," she said with a grin.

"It stands for Gorgeous Girl, which you certainly are. Also, GG has a slightly naughty French flair to it, which you certainly have."

They both laughed. Then she impulsively threw her arms around his shoulders. "It could be good between us," she said wistfully.

"It already is," he whispered.

It was time to return to Alnwyk.

She looked into his eyes. "It could work for us, Paul. I know it could."

"No, it never would, my dear. But our friendship will be a very satisfying thing. Now let's go meet Bill and talk about Poland."

♦

That night when they finished their discussion, everyone was certain that they understood the time frame for every item on the trip.

"Paul, will you stay another moment? " Bill asked. "I've got one more question for you."

"Of course."

They walked outdoors so that no one could hear their conversation.

Bill said that he had set a trap. "I have a safe here in the drawing room of this castle. No one has the combination to it but me."

"But someone opened it last night. Am I right?"

Bill nodded. "What the thief found in the safe was a copy of a report to Churchill which talked about two things. The first point mentioned that we have already arranged for the secret plans to go back to England. The second talks about the group's responsibility for guarding de Wiart at the Jasna Gora Monastery activities next week. It said that we are in the midst of establishing a security plan for de Wiart next week."

Paul smiled. "Good. Your fake letter to Churchill was a great idea. With it we may be discouraging the Nazis from any action at all to steal the plans."

"Possibly, and that would be good. But if they accept the fact that it is futile to look for the plans, they might be willing to settle on revenge. They may decide to destroy de Wiart as a symbol of Polish resistance. If that is what they decide, security for de Wiart next week at Jasna Gora is going to be very difficult."

Paul said, "I know. Count on us to do it properly."

"I do. So does Winston Churchill."

Paul wondered how much longer it would be before that confidence was tested.

Chapter 10

"It's time to begin," Paul said. There was no strain in his voice, but rather, a strong desire to "be at it," as he said.

It was early Sunday morning and the group had gathered in the library at Alnwyk for one last meeting before they left.

"I have a surprise for you," said Bill. He flipped a switch on his desk. "Sir Androz de Wiart wants to talk to you for a moment," he explained.

De Wiart's voice boomed as he gave his personal thanks to each of them for making the upcoming visit to Poland. "We appreciate anything you can do to help us," he said. He would see them soon in Poland. "Thank you," he said again before the telephone connection ended.

"Sandra's flight will leave first," Stephenson said after de Wiart's call. She would be traveling on a Polish air force plane, rather than the commercial flight which Paul, Harry, and David would take two hours after Sandra's plane had left.

"Sandra, your flight will land at one of the countless small governmental airports that surround Krakow," Bill explained. "Use the room we've reserved for you at the Karmel Hotel for Sunday night. That way Walter Schellenberg won't know where you are until you check into the Hotel Amadeus on Monday morning. That's where Schellenberg is expecting you to be."

Bill stopped talking and looked around at the group. "Let me explain the Schellenberg connection to all of you. It's a very important component of this assignment. Sandra has led Schellenberg to believe that she has access to information about this mission that he wants. As you know, we have tried to establish the fact that a fictitious Polish scientist recently died unexpectedly. This was someone who gossip said had invented something that would guarantee success for the Nazis in the upcoming war. Your group is supposedly traveling to Poland to bring back to Great Britain Jan Babij's detailed plans for jet propulsion engines for use in military plans and weapons. The story we established is that Jan died before he could get his plans out of Poland. Since a war is fast approaching, members of the Polish resistance are working with us to organize our plans to retrieve his work."

He paused. "We've also started a new rumor that is beginning to make the rounds. That is that the scientific papers at Krakow may have already been given to the British. You see, the emphasis here is to keep the balloons up in the air. In other words, keep the Nazis confused about the real disposition of those papers for as long as possible. We want them confused about whether to continue looking or whether to stop."

He looked at Paul. "According to the story we've concocted, you, Paul, posing as Charles Scott Devereau, and Harry Paine and Dave Christie, your friends who came to Poland with you, will be picked up at the airport by Tomas and Sofia Janusek, a couple that allegedly rented their house to Jan. Actually, the Januseks are a couple in the Polish resistance working for De Wiart. Follow their directions exactly for playing the part of the cousin and friends of the dead man. Once you are at Jan's home you will be told when the emphasis of your mission will shift to the protection of de Wiart at the Jasna Gorna Monastery."

"Remember, all of you," he said as he looked around at them one last time before they left. "Lieutenant General De Wiart's soldiers will be constantly shadowing you for backup.

All of you know how to contact De Wiart's people in an emergency. You can instantly get a signal through to DeWiart. He will provide help."

Sandra could feel Paul's eyes on her. She decided that he was probably visualizing the way that she had gotten Schellenberg involved in the phony plan. She felt her face flush. He never would understand her. But did it matter? She was surprised by her own emotions, for if she were honest, she would have to confess that it did, at least as far as Paul was concerned.

Finally the last question about the mission had been asked and answered.

It was time to go.

♦

Sandra sat back in her airplane seat after takeoff. She watched the ground gradually fade away and soon she saw nothing but the clouds that covered the sky. Great Britain had disappeared. Would she ever be returning? She discovered that although she felt pain in leaving a country she loved, she was also sad about the attitudes of many of the British who sought appeasement. But then where was it that she wanted to be? Was there any place in this world that believed values to be more important than money? She wasn't certain that there was.

"Please follow me," the air attendant said softly to her.

Without a word Sandra followed him to the front of the plane and to an area behind the front cabin. When the attendant knocked the door opened. Sandra stepped in quickly and then closed the door. The tall man sitting next to the door locked it after she entered. He was a thin man who sat regally, even in the cramped seat of the airplane.

"Sasha," he said. He drew her close to him. "You will always be my Sasha, not the Sandra which we Brits call you."

"But it doesn't matter, does it, Uncle Androz? You are as dear to me now as you were when I was a child."

Max Rosenberg and Androz De Wiart had become friends in South Africa during the Boer War, around 1900. Both the same age, their friendship had continued until the end of Max's life in 1932. It was a friendship which joined them in fighting to save the lives of the millions of the poor throughout Europe whose lives no one seemed to want to save.

" 'Always listen to Androz, Sasha.' I can't remember how many times Max repeated that to me during his life," Sandra said. "He always told me what a good man you were, and how there weren't too many around like you. Max was right," Sandra said. She looked at Androz with tears in her eyes. "I've been a muck up, I suspect. I need advice from you. All of it will be assiduously accepted and followed."

She stopped to blow her nose and catch her breath. "It's this approaching war. All of us who have any sense want to scream and shout to the idiots who are leading us into war. But nothing works, Uncle Androz. No one is listening."

"I know. No one ever listens. Why can't you accept that as a given?"

"But you've always fought for what you believed in." She knew the price that he had paid. "Look at you. You look like an elegant pirate, with that one eye that was shot out and the left hand you lost in World War I. You've never been afraid to sacrifice, have you?"

It was difficult for him to explain himself to her. "I knew that I had no choice. As Churchill said, we will only win by sacrificing. From the highest to the humblest sacrifice, all are of equal honor during a time of war. But let's talk about someone I love—you. You worry me. I thought about what you are doing to get information for Stephenson and about the services you will perform for the SOE when war begins."

He looked at her carefully, formulating his words before he spoke them. "I think you lack the right credentials for both whoring and for sending people to their death."

He added quickly, "As well as the right temperament."

She wanted to say something, but wasn't certain what it was.

"I'm certain that my friend Max would say the same thing," he said. There was a long silence. He opened his briefcase and pulled out a papers. "After you told me about Walter Schellenberg I had his office searched. We found this and made a copy of it for you. I am only letting you see this because of what he said are his feelings for you."

Sandra opened the packet with a sinking feeling in her stomach. She had an intuition that it wasn't good. And it wasn't. Someone had copied the pages in Walter's scrapbook that were devoted to her. She read how he had described her and then quickly put the pages down.

"I have no difficulty believing this." She told him about her phone call to Schellenberg the next morning after she met with him. "The man who answered Walter's phone asked if there was a message that I wanted to leave for him. He called me 'Miss Hoover' and I didn't correct him. The name was familiar. I think that a woman of that name works as a secretary in the German Embassy in London. I bet she is one of his girlfriends," Sandra said with bitterness.

"I'll find out." DeWiart changed the subject. "How much do you remember about your childhood, Sasha?"

"Most of it, I suppose. The good and the bad."

"What about your memories of Max?"

"They are loving ones," she said carefully.

"Tell me what you remember about Max's activities. Was he only involved in business?"

She was puzzled about where he was going with this. "No, Max had many activities. We never knew the complete extent of what he did. Nor did he seem to want us to know."

"That's because much of his life after his twenties was devoted to Zionism."

She looked surprised.

De Wiart said, "You must always remember that there was a fast growth of anti-Semitism in Europe during Max's early years. The world called it the 'Jewish problem,' blaming the Jews for any economic crisis which arose."

"But Max was a good businessman who made his money ethically."

"He certainly did. And so did most Jews. Not only that, but Max spent much of it on the poor wandering Jews in Europe who were being thrown out of every country they tried to enter. For example, since 1867 Romania has passed 196 laws that deny rights to Jews. Max was one of the few who helped the Jewish masses—the Russians, the Slavs, the French—anyone who was a victim of anti-Semitism in Europe to escape. And he did something else wonderful for them, in addition to loaning money to as many worthy people as he could. Intolerance, fanaticism, and cruelty can all be overcome when one can fight them one by one. But when Max saw all these awful traits coming at one time he knew that it was time for the oppressed to leave."

She looked at him quizzically.

"He became one of the leading Zionists of his times. Giving his own money wasn't enough, in his estimation. By 1895 he was traveling to places such as Vienna, Berlin, Paris, and London in an effort to gain financial support from Europe's wealthiest Jews for his idea to establish a Jewish homeland. Not all of his efforts were successful, though. It seems that many had ideas for a potential Jewish homeland that were

different from his choice of Palestine as the homeland for Jews. That confusion happened because the peace talk held by the world after World War I often redrew the maps and forced people to leave the countries they had lived in for centuries. Millions of Jews now had no "country of origin," and were helplessly limited to living within different borders or were excluded from all countries. By the 1930's anti-Semitism was widely seen by many countries as actually being patriotic, with spiritual backing from some churches. This even happened, unfortunately, in Great Britain because of the growth of unreasoning hatred toward the Jews by the dictators who were emerging. Max became friendly with such Jewish leaders as Herzl, Chaim-Weizmann, and David Ben-Gurion in order to help promote Zionism."

Sandra said, "I remember how Romanian border guards would give my father exit passes for many poor peasants when Max bribed them. I also remember that as a teenager I often accompanied Max to help the people dressed as peasant barrow pushers who were trying to escape their fate. Max would follow them by boldly driving a Mercedes-Benz that impressed the border guards with his wealth."

De Wiart smiled at the recollections. "But the situation is getting worse as war gets closer. Even Great Britain is now beginning to renege on the Balfour Declaration and is seeking to limit Jewish migration to Israel, in spite of the fact that millions of Jews will probably die in the concentration camps that Hitler is constructing, even as we speak."

"I know," she said.

"You might want to join in the same work that Max did. Can you accept, as I do, that one's individual destiny remains linked, whatever one does, with a collective destiny when it is a question of an entire people struggling for their survival and

"After we return from Poland, let's talk about it, Uncle Androz."

"We will talk. But back to this mission. You understand exactly what your time schedule is?

You will arrive late tonight. Monday you will spend in Krakow by yourself, and Tuesday morning you will meet with Schellenberg. When you meet with Walter on Tuesday, I want you to do exactly as I tell you. Right?"

She nodded.

"Max will be proud of you."

"I hope you will be, too."

"Now listen very carefully. . … "

♦

When Sandra left the cabin de Wiart felt exhausted, but elated as well.

Their plan was worrying the Nazis. It was evident that they had no idea of the smuggling activity that would soon happen in Warsaw. He had used Sandra well. Their plan would work. He had no doubt about that. And its success would save many lives.

His plan would work.

♦

Already in Poland, Walter Schellenberg was not happy as he read the report that had just been submitted to him. Rumors were swirling in Krakow that the jet propulsion plans of Jan Babij were already in England. However, those rumors could not be confirmed.

"Damn." Was he wasting his time looking for the plans? Although he would like to know as soon as possible, Walter decided to postpone any decision about what to do until he spoke to Sandra. She might still come through for him, although he doubted it.

Chapter 11

"You can take my aisle seat," Paul said to Harry when he saw Harry's face turning quickly into interesting variations of gray. "Just keep talking to me and don't look out the window," counseled Paul, who blamed himself for Harry's condition. How could he have been so inconsiderate not to remember that Harry hated to fly and got sick every time he did? To keep his friend's mind occupied Paul quickly started a spirited discussion about all the good times they had shared during their times in Poland. It did distract Harry slightly, at least enough to prevent many of those hurried trips to the washroom that Harry was famous for.

However, they all had heavy hearts. Very soon the commercial plane that they were flying would land in Krakow. The thought of being in Poland, usually looked forward to, was tempered today by the knowledge that the utter destruction of this small country was probably going to occur within a matter of days. Indeed, it would happen whenever the Nazis decided to make it happen. *Goddamn the Nazis and their fucking leader* was what Paul wanted to shout to everyone on their crowded plane. However, he knew he couldn't, since nothing that he was thinking was permissible according to the laws of any country in the world. Instead, he had to be content with glaring at those on the plane who looked as if they might have German blood and inwardly cursing them, their ancestors, and anyone who

As for David, he sat at the back of the plane, pretending to be asleep but really tracking the other passengers very carefully to see if there was any interest in Paul and Harry. David's assignment for this trip would be to cover Paul and whoever was with him.

During the flight they were careful not to say anything much that was important for fear of being overheard.

At one point Paul said, "I'm glad we're here."

Harry responded with bitterness. "This will probably be our last visit for a while. If there even is a Poland after Hitler."

"You are probably right," admitted Paul. "Look around. I don't see many happy faces, do you?" He lowered his voice. "Since we don't know how everyone feels about the Nazis, it may be wise to lower your voice a little."

Both agreed that Poland had always seemed to them to be a country which demanded healthy, vigorous people who were not afraid to work hard. But it had always been a beautiful country.

"Poland and Germany have always been my favorite places for spectacular views, and now look at what is inevitable for both of them," said Paul. He looked out of the airplane window, staring blankly at nothing, but thinking that all the historical wrongs and atrocities which the world could inflict had already been experienced by the Poles. "Poor Poland," he whispered softly.

He knew that throughout history Polish borders have changed almost continuously. Geographically squeezed between the two huge aggressive powers of Germany and Russia, as well as by other smaller but aggressive countries, the beautiful country of Poland has repeatedly been invaded and fought over since the beginning of history. Its beginning as a

Then, for 150 years the Piast dynasty ruled the country and embroiled the nation in frequent domestic quarrels. In 1385 a treaty with Lithuania initiated a process of consolidation between these two countries. Ultimately Poland's political and military history led to its being partitioned by Russia, Prussia, and Austria. By 1795 Poland had effectively been wiped off the map of Europe, a situation which would continue for more than 100 years. So complete was this obliteration that Polish attempts to achieve independence by insurrection were always unsuccessful. It was not until 1918 that Poland regained its sovereignty.

And now in 1939 the Nazis were about to invade Poland.

"I know what you are thinking," Harry said to Paul. "Horrible, isn't it? And soon to start, if Hitler gets his way. Poles may be very proud of Warsaw, the Polish city that rivals any of the huge European centers, but I think their real love is Krakow. Krakow has traditionally been one of the major centers of Polish culture. Think about music or any of the arts. It's all in Krakow."

"I did some graduate work here at Krakow's Jagiellonian University many years after my work at Oxford," Paul said. "Living here was a feast." That "feast" was about to end abruptly, Paul was afraid. He wished they had more time. How wonderful it would have been to explore once more such areas as Krakow's Old Town, an area which proudly traced its history from 1257. But it was too late.

They wouldn't have any spare time for anything, He knew that. Their total concentration must be on making this mission a success.

♦

Their plane circled Krakow, getting ready for its final approach to the city.

They landed on time. That should mean that Tomas and Sofia Janusek would be waiting for them. The airport was busy, full of serious faces rushing to the airline counters as soon as possible to board their planes. *If I weren't on this mission, I, too, would be rushing to leave Poland now that Hitler's troops are on their way,* Paul thought. He saw nervous, jumpy faces, rather than happy tourists eagerly awaiting a vacation.

Just so, thought Paul as a short, stocky man and a taller but equally stocky woman approached them after they had passed through the airport exit gate with their suitcases. Paul had remembered to pin an i.d. tag on his jacket to make the task of the Januseks easier.

"Did you have a good trip?" asked Tomas Janusek. "May I see your id. cards, please?" He was courteous. "It's just a formality, of course," he apologized. He introduced himself and his wife and then repeated each person's name carefully so that he might say it properly. De Wiart had told them that the Januseks would check their identification papers.

"Just so," said Mrs. Janusek. She was trying to speak English to them, but it was difficult to understand her.

Paul looked at Tomas and said, "We all speak Polish. It would probably be easier for her to speak in her own language."

Tomas looked sad. "She is recovering from a stroke. Her speech hasn't come back yet. Speak to me rather than to her," he said in English. "I like to practice my English. We don't have many English coming to Krakow anymore."

Paul whispered to Harry when the Januseks walked ahead of them to find their car in the airport parking lot. "I don't want to be critical, but Tomas' Polish has a strange accent. But then again, who am I to judge?"

Out of the corner of his eye Paul had watched David stop at the auto rental window where a dark blue car reserved for him by one of de Wiart's men had been driven out of the car lot and sat waiting for David to drive it away.

In no time at all Paul and Harry were seated in the back seat of the Janusek's roomy old black sedan. Because they had brought only small overnight suitcases with them so that they could travel light, there was no difficulty in fitting the suitcases in the huge trunk at the back of the Janusek car. Finally they were settled and ready.

Their assignment in Poland was about to begin. Paul's juices were flowing because of the challenge that lay ahead of him.

"Would you like me to point out things on the trip to our home in Bielany? This is a beautiful part of Poland," Tomas told them before he started the car.

They assured him that they would.

Soon they were rolling along the road, one which rapidly was becoming a rural one as soon as they reached the outskirts of the city of Krakow. Paul began to pay close attention when he remembered something which de Wiart had told them on Sunday. He had said that they were to stop at a gas station on Route 75, approximately one mile past the Route 40 turnoff. According to de Wiart, the Januseks had been told to stop there to confirm that everything was going right on plan.

It didn't take long for that gas station to appear.

As they rounded the last curve, Paul could see it on their left side. But Tomas was not making any effort to stop the car. When Paul saw Harry start to say something, he shook his head slightly. *No*, thought Paul. *Let's see what the Januseks will do.*

Their car whizzed right past the gas station. Tomas had completely ignored de Wiart's instructions to stop at that gas station so that de Wiart might speak to Paul and Harry. Their plan had been compromised even before it started.

Paul's mind went into overdrive.

When he saw a mountain lookout area coming up on their side of the road. He said, "Tomas, would you stop at that scenic lookout? I'd like to take a longer look at this beautiful scenery."

"Of course," said Tomas.

A quick look behind them comforted Paul. There was no dark blue rental car behind then with David at the wheel. According to de Wiart's directions, if David saw their car zip past the gas station he had been instructed to stop at that gas station in order to tell de Wiart what had happened.

But what did all this mean?

It meant that the Januseks with them were Nazis, not the real Januseks, Paul concluded. That was what it meant.

As soon as he could, Paul edged closer to a back tire of the Janusek car. With the excuse that he had dropped something, he bent over and quickly rammed the knife which he always carried on his key chain into the tire. He was the one who looked at the tire in a few minutes and said, "We have a flat, Tomas." Then, when David passed by he saw the signal of emergency Paul was making and pulled into the lookout.

Paul shook his head slightly at Dave. *You don't know us,* the look said. Realizing the truth about the Januseks, just as Paul had done, Dave had donned a hat and kept his head down so that the Januseks would not be able to recognize him later if they met.

"I'll be glad to take you and the tire down back to the gas station," Dave said to Paul.

Finally they were back on the road after their trip back to the gas station.

The tire had been fixed, and best of all, Paul had used the opportunity to speak to de Wiart who was waiting for him in the men's room at the gas station.

From de Wiart he learned that the Januseks who had picked them up at the airport must be Nazis who knew nothing about the safety measures de Wiart had established for the drive. De Wiart said that the real Januseks had probably been kidnapped.

"I would wager that the house which the dead man is supposed to have rented from the Januseks has been completely searched by now," de Wiart said. "But that's good. It will tease the Nazis about the story we invented. The real Januseks are probably tied up in the other house which the authentic Januseks live in. It is about a mile from the rental house. We'll get them out all right. This does mean, however, that Schellenberg is working hard to find out what is important about this Krakow mission of ours. But I have a feeling that he has found nothing. Last week we made sure that the rental house of the dead man looked as if he had really lived there. However, nothing of value was left for someone like Schellenberg to find. Right now Schellenberg must be wondering if the "secret plans" we have teased him with are already out of the country."

Paul wondered if this new information about the Januseks meant that the plans for the mission should be changed.

"No," said the general. "Go back with the couple to the rental home as if nothing has happened. If there are any changes to be made, I'll let you know. However, I want you to know that the Nazis have bugged the house in Bielany. But that is what we want. If you need to share information with each other, be sure to go outside where it would be impossible to bug your conversations. Let me explain."

De Wiart looked very soberly at Paul. "I have something very important to tell you," he said gravely. "I learned not long ago that the plans of the Polish government for smuggling a secret out of Poland and giving it to England have to be moved up. It seems that there isn't as much more time left as we had thought until the Germans attack." He looked at Paul, saying,

"We must soon stage a fake smuggling in Bielany in order to divert the attention of the Germans from the real mission."

""How soon is soon?" Paul asked, although he was afraid that he already knew the answer.

"Late tonight," answered de Wiart. "I will tell you briefly what we will do."

Actually, the role that Paul, Harry, and Dave would play was uncomplicated. "The first thing that you must do is to take advantage of the fact that the house is bugged," said de Wiart. "Talk openly about the fact that some Polish resistance workers in a four-door black sedan will stop by the house at 2 am tonight to pick up two boxes of plans and papers that are hidden in the Bielany chalet where you are staying. I will tell you where the boxes are hidden before you leave. Make up a story that the resistance workers have plans to take these boxes to de Wiart who, along with other Resistance workers, will be staying at a safe house in Krakow. Be sure to say that de Wiart plans to have the files flown out of Poland from a Resistance airport in the area."

De Wiart looked at Paul. "Shortly before two am, the three of you are to carry these two boxes outside to a driveway on the left side of the house. A black sedan will pull up and you will help the driver, a man well known for being a resistance leader in Krakow, and his assistant to load the boxes into the car."

Paul said, "I understand where this plan is headed. Because the Nazis know what is to happen since the house is bugged, they will follow the sedan, rather than stealing the boxes here. For if they wait until the car reaches the safe house, they can capture not only the files, but also you and your followers."

"Right," said de Wiart. "However, I can assure you that the car with the fake boxes of plans will never reach our safe house. Wouldn't it be ironic if the car, loaded with gallons of gasoline, accidentally caught fire on the way to Krakow, burning the car and the boxes inside to a crisp as well as the two corpses we placed in the car much earlier? Of course the driver and his assistant will have jumped from the car before it begins its fiery ascent down a steep hill. We will have another car hidden in the woods waiting to pick them up."

Paul smiled. "I can't think of anything sadder for Schellenberg. How close he was to getting the glory he wanted. How sad to be defeated by something as simple as an act of nature."

De Wiart said, "And now let's get on the road to Bielany and get the plan started." He turned to Paul. "Sandra is not to know about the 2 pm pickup."

Paul nodded. He turned to de Wiart in admiration. "I respect the way you plan, sir."

"Thank you. Just wish me luck that everything works."

♦

The rest of the ride to Bielany, a village approximately eight miles from the Krakow city center, was uneventful, other than that Tomas attempted to make them believe that he and the woman were the authentic Januseks by trying to sound knowledgeable about this area of Poland. From the fake Tomas they learned that the Bielany suburb was one of the most beautiful areas of Poland, thanks to the beautiful Wolski Forest which borders the area. On its southern part which faces the Vistula River they saw the awe-inspiring Silver Mountain, an area which contains the mighty Church and Hermitage of t the Camaldolese Monks.

Tomas pointed to the huge monastery as they passed by. "It is a religious order with very strict monastic rules," he said. The monastery was spectacularly situated. "Of course, this church is only about a third of the size of the monastery in Czestochowa which houses the Black Madonna painting."

"How far are we from the home you rented to Jan?" asked Paul.

"Easy walking distance," Tomas said.

"If we have a few minutes tonight we'd like to take a walk and see the monastery," Paul said. That might be a good excuse for them to see the area around the house in case they had to leave quickly, Paul thought.

"You will enjoy the walk. Look, we're almost at our house," Tomas said.

They had just left one road and were turning into the outskirts of a little village that was ahead.

Their car finished the steep twisting climb and regained its speed on the road leading round the western side of a long narrow road which skirted a small but peaceful lake. Halfway up the lake the road ended and they saw a little village which welcomed them. Rather than being a usual resort-type village which welcomed tourists, this village gave the appearance of having been unoccupied for a long time. It probably was, for as Harry asked Paul, how many people would vacation at a spot which had the threat of Hitler hanging over their heads?

"Not many," answered Paul.

The Januseks were silent, obviously disapproving of what Harry had said before they remembered to erase the looks of disapproval from their faces for the sake of the English visitors.

At the end of the area sat a small hotel which gave the impression of being deserted. Several wooden cabins were on either side of the hotel. These, too, were empty and quiet.

"It isn't a good tourist season, is it?" said Paul.

Tomas shook his head.

Behind the hotel, in the large sweep of meadows stretching back to the wooded mountains in the background, lay a row of larger wooden peasant houses. A small boat floated quietly in the waters around the pier.

"That is where we live," Tomas said, pointing to one of the houses.

"How neat everything is," remarked Paul.

"Almost as if everyone were dead," said Harry.

"Or will be soon," Paul said in a whisper that the Januseks couldn't hear.

"Soon we'll see the house that Jan rented from us. It isn't far from here," said Tomas.

Tomas had slowed down so that two large cows could slowly walk toward their car, each of their steps creating a tinkling sound of the bells around their necks. Behind the animals were three children who guided the cows while they flicked flies from the faces of the animals.

Tomas now chose another road which led them to a group of trees surrounding a house. It was in the middle of a broad green meadow on the sheltered side of a small hill, the side which had been hidden from them on their ride to the house. It was an isolated site, for there was no sign of any life in the wooded valley below it or on any of the mountains which walled in the valley. Below the car huge trees completely blocked the house from public view.

Its isolation had made it a perfect place to build a house. "Did you and your wife design it?" asked Paul.

Tomas shook his head. "We bought it already built ten years ago as an investment."

At least the impersonators are able to think quickly about their answers, thought Paul.

Paul saw that the valley area was misting because of the nearby mountains, even though the wind had died down. There were no sounds at all to be heard.

"This is where we park," Tomas said. "Take your luggage with you."

When they got out of the car they saw a track that would take them across to the front entrance of the house. It wasn't a large house, but its two stories looked sturdily built with stout overhanging eaves and outdoor patios.

"The house was probably built by a wealthy person who used it for summers," Paul guessed.

"Welcome to *Jezioro Zajazd,*" said Tomas.

"Dziekuje," answered Paul, glad that his Polish was very fluent.

Before they started walking to the house they heard another greeting.

"Welcome to *Jezioro Zajazd."* Everyone stared in surprise, for this last welcome had come from a man with a gun in his pocket who now stood in front of them.

"I apologize if I have frightened you," the man said. "De Wiart sent me here to take these two German sympathizers away." He pointed at the two Janusek imposters. "May I introduce the real Januseks?" This time he pointed to a man and woman who were walking up the driveway. He said, "We will take these two away."

With that he left as quietly as they had arrived. Within minutes the real Januseks joined them.

"You are probably hungry after your flight," said Tomas. "My wife will prepare a meal for you," he said. "Meanwhile, choose the bedroom each of you wants from those on the second floor."

Before they entered the house, Paul called his group aside and explained what he learned from his meeting with de Wiart. He told them what to say for the benefit of the Nazis who were bugging the house.

As much as he could, Paul attempted to familiarize himself with the interior of the house after they finished the meal Sofia prepared for them. Who knows? Knowledge about the house might save their lives if they had to get out of here quickly. He also seized an opportunity to ask Harry to walk outside with him in order to see a beautiful view. What Paul wanted was a few minutes so that he could explain to Harry more about what had happened at the gas station. As for Dave, as instructed he had driven to the home of a friend of de Wiart 's in the area. He would be watching over the house tonight.

Paul and Harry walked around the first floor later after the authentic Januseks left for their home. It was a pleasant area, seemingly a man's room with its smells of pine and tobacco. And its comfortable leather furniture centered around the open fireplace. The room had a piano and piles of music scores casually placed on top. Jan Babij might well have lived here. *If there had been a Jan Babij,* Paul thought. He was eager to get started, even slightly nervous. But wasn't that expected? Had he ever undertaken a mission like the one Bill Stephenson had just given him?

Enough worrying, Paul told himself. Tonight he, Dave, and Harry would continue the job of convincing the Nazis that they were here to steal the plans for Babij' s supposed jet propulsion work.

At that, he had a sudden thought about Sandra Martin. He had a premonition that she might not be able to fool Walter Schellenberg in her Krakow meeting with him. From what Paul had learned, Schellenberg was much smarter than she, although Sandra seemed equally devious. Would she be able to convince Walter that she was giving him accurate information about the mission? He wanted to believe that she could work Schellenberg the way that they wanted. But he wasn't certain that he believed what he was saying. He had doubts about her, although for the life of him he couldn't explain why.

He and Harry took a short walk outside. "Be ready and dressed by 1:45 am so we can get the boxes in that car when it pulls up," Paul said to Harry. "I wish that we were going on that ride to the fake safe house."

"It should be quite a ride if de Wiart has planned it," answered Harry.

Chapter 12

Sandra pushed and pushed while the rental car clutch squeaked and squeaked. Finally, the car agreed to move into third gear, almost as a grudging courtesy to her. She looked at her watch, telling herself that she might still be on time at the Hotel Amadeus, even though she certainly had no desire to be on time for this particular meeting with Walter.

It had been a busy morning for her, as well as a productive one in Krakow. She had chosen three new candidates for SOE training. They were good choices. She knew that. And yet she felt sorrow in her heart about her decisions. When the war arrived she would have trained them by then to parachute into Nazi-occupied Poland to commit sabotage. And what then? The odds were that they would be dead before they had served a month in the SOE.

The busy morning had also accomplished another goal of taking her mind off what would soon happen—her meeting with Walter. How she had agonized about it. Now it was here.

If she had her wish, it would be merely a matter of falling into his arms and letting her feelings for him take over. But never again would there be a time when she would fall into his arms. She had decided that. More correctly, she wasn't going to ever let it happen again with him.

No, she told herself. *Never.*

She tried to take her mind off it by remembering that soon in a matter of hours she would be with Paul and the group. It helped a little.

She and Walter arrived at the lobby of the Amadeus Hotel at about the same time. Other than a surprised look which both of them suppressed at seeing the other, one would have thought them to be strangers as each stepped into the same elevator. Walter, however, got off at the sixth floor, allowing her some time to enter her seventh floor suite and take the lock off the door so that Walter might enter quickly.

And what about that word "never," the word she had just chosen to express her intentions toward him? When he arrived it soon became "No, please," a phrase said as calmly as she could when he entered the room and strode to her side. In turn, that phrase then transfigured itself into a sentence. "We have a great deal to talk about and a tight schedule in which to do it." she told him, her feelings as transparent as such a sentence can make them.

However, that sentence ended just as weakly as most sentences do. Ultimately he pushed, she lost her desire to protest, and then within five seconds she had led him to the bedroom where they soon were having sex once again. And great sex, at that.

Afterwards, she dressed quickly before dissolving into tears and trembling as she clung to him. It was clear that her "no" had rapidly deteriorated into a rather spineless "I never wanted that to happen" sentence that she whined, rather than said.

"Of course you did," he said, busily zipping up his trouser fly as she whined away.

His demeanor had changed, though. Obviously confused, he could not hide a look of irritation at what Sandra interpreted as frustration with his inability to control this situation and frustration about her inability to tell him what he wanted.

"What is wrong with you?" he asked, trying to pin her down.

She smiled wanly at that. "It's probably more a question of what is right rather than what is wrong," she said.

"Stop dabbling in semantics, Sandra. Your knowledge in that area is also very weak." His tone was sharp.

She said, "I take it that you've decided not to waste your charms on me. Right?"

He ignored her words and got to the point. "Do your nonsensical remarks mean that you don't love me enough to have found out information for me about the jet propulsion plans?"

"There you go. That is all you care about, isn't it, Walter?"

"You happen to be right. But that doesn't matter. Are you going to give me any information, Sandra? I'll get it even without your help, you know. And once I do, what will happen to you? He paused for emphasis. "You can be sure that I will make your life as miserable as possible."

It took all of her courage not to be shaken by his words. But she wouldn't give Walter that satisfaction. She would say what she had been instructed to say. "I'm sure that you would like to make my life miserable. But fortunately you won't. Now let me tell you why." She moved closer to him so that her eyes stared up into his.

However, all her control rapidly disappeared. She heard herself screaming like a fishwife. "You are not going to get one more bit of information from me. Find out everything yourself, Walter. What you want will probably leave Bielany tonight. It won't matter. You are going to be the loser in this assignment. All I can see are two options open to you at this point."

"Really?" His tone was unconcerned.

That certainly didn't frighten him, she thought, after having searched his eyes to see if she could find a flicker of fear in them. She didn't. Although she wanted nothing more than to wipe that sarcasm off his face, she would try to maintain an emotional distance while she did it.

"Yes. Really," she said angrily, although the anger was more directed at herself for allowing him to provoke her than it was at him.

"And what are my options, if I might ask."

"The first is to pack your suitcase, pick up all the Nazi goons you brought with you to Poland, and then go back to Berlin. If you do I'll never tell your bosses Himmler and Hitler what a horse's ass you have been."

"And the second?" She could see the smile on his face that he was trying to stifle. That will change soon, she thought.

"The second option isn't very nice. It will be one where you unsuccessfully try to find the secret plans. You really can't do that, because they are probably already on the way out of here, and right under your nose. Once we're back in London the German Ambassador to Great Britain will receive a package from the British Ambassador. The package will contain some interesting material. This includes the photos you once showed me of your maternal grandparents. Remember the photo that had a Jewish star in the background? What a careless mistake you made in showing me that. It made me do some research in depth. You will really like the information I found. It includes a copy of a marriage certificate issued by the synagogue in Luxembourg where your grandparents married as well as the address of the nursing home where your grandfather still lives."

Walter attempted a bluff. "Is that all? Lots of Nazis have some Jewish roots. All that is necessary is to renounce one's ancestors."

"My dear Walter, have you any idea how many people you have stepped on in your rise to the top? I am sure that there are many who would love to use this information about you. But that's not all I know about you. The German ambassador will also find some tapes that he might want Himmler and Hitler to listen to. The tapes are wonderfully fascinating examples of pillow talk in which you really have said some interesting things about your bosses to me. All the wonderfully new German technology about voice recognition will prove that you are the one speaking on those tapes. I certainly have been improving my technical skills, haven't I?"

After that he had nothing more to say.

But she did.

"You may contemplate killing me. A word of advice. Don't do it. I am well guarded. Kill me and you will go next." Her voice was now confident. De Wiart had promised her that she would be protected and that was all the assurance she needed.

She walked to the door and opened it. She said, "Goodby, Walter. Here's hoping that you decide not to bother me anymore." Then she got serious. "I'm very sorry, for I have to admit that I do love you. Today was better than ever. But that is my problem, isn't it?"

When he walked out she locked the door. She quickly finished dressing and closed her suitcase. As she looked around the room, she realized that her anger against Walter had diminished, but not disappeared. He deserved what she had said. Sandra allowed herself to wallow for a few minutes in the righteous feeling shared by all those who say too much. She had been courageous in her words, hadn't she? She had certainly said what she was supposed to say, hadn't she? Of course, one might rightly suspect that Sandra had forgotten the truth of the old adage which warns us that whom the gods would destroy they must first make angry.

When she left her room and arrived in the lobby a large group of travelers were checking in.

Sandra panicked while attempting to cross through the impatient group. Memory suddenly overcame her, and the adult she was became a child again who had just been separated from her father in another lobby at another time. She was alone once more. Her father had disappeared. Once more she was overcome by the same despair she had felt those years ago. Once more she wanted to scream for her father.

Years ago, she had quickly become happy again when her father suddenly reappeared to take her into his arms. "You will be all right, my dear," he said over and over to stop her tears.

But today, there was no one to hold her and to love her when she opened her eyes. The only faces she saw today were those of impatient travelers who looked at her strangely.

"I am not all right," she cried out to those who walked a little faster away from her when they heard her words.

However, her panic passed when she rested for a minute. De Wiart had a better car waiting for Sandra. She checked out quickly and threw her suitcase into the trunk.

She was off to Bielany and Paul.

While she drove she thought about what she had just said to Walter.

Served him right, she thought. He had never loved her. She saw his proud, handsome face in her mind's eye and longed to be able to touch it. But it was also a selfish and cruel face. She knew that. *But after all was said and done,* as the ballad said, *there was really only one. And Walter, Walter, it's you. But I can forget you*, she vowed. She would do it in the name of refusing to become his victim.

Sandra's foot slammed down hard on the gas pedal as she concentrated on her driving. All of the natural beauty of this area of Poland was passing by too quickly for her to appreciate the history and the charm of Krakow, with its streets of multicolored townhouses radiating out from an enchanting market square. That was sad, for Krakow was a place to be enjoyed. Proud of its intellectual background as a town that had paved the way for the Renaissance, its most famous student at that time had been

Nicholaus Copernicus. The magnificent Tatra mountains where the area's starkly beautiful alpine mountains were beginning their climb—all of this went unappreciated today by Sandra as she sped to Bielany and her friends. Krakow was an invitation to see beauty. *But not today,* she thought with sadness. *I'll be back, That's a promise.* As for Krakow, it wasn't certain whether it would be there to have that promise fulfilled.

Suddenly a voice spoke to her from the back seat. "Pull off the road as soon as you can," it directed. Her hands became icy cold and she did as she was told. When she attempted to turn around to see who sat in her back seats she received a slight crack on the head with the gun the man held in his hands.

"What do you want?" she cried.

"Pull over to the side." When she did he continued. "Here's what we want. Listen carefully because I am going to tell you what I will do to you if you ever make any attempt again to blackmail or harm *Brigadefuhre*r Schellenberg." The voice then itemized in detail what would be done to her before she died.

Although she tried, Sandra was unable to stop the sudden gush of bile that poured out of her mouth. The man waited patiently for the spasms to pass.

"I promise," she screamed. "Please believe me."

He looked at her with bewilderment. "Oh, no, I wouldn't believe anything you said. But do believe what I say. You see, I will enjoy every moment of pain that I cause you. I will stretch it out so that you will long to die. I hope you do tell someone about the *Brigadefuhrer* because I would enjoy torturing you. Now let me get out here. You go on to your friends."

Sandra gunned the car once more onto the road after he got out of the car. She saw little of the road, intent only on getting as far away as she could. She began to calm down.

Finally she reached the village after The Church and Hermitage of the Camaldolese Monks came into sight, just as Paul had told her it would. She had no trouble following his clear directions to the Janusek house where everyone was staying. However, once she arrived she sat in the car for a few minutes to ensure that she looked calm. Inside she was shaking.

Had the gunman told the truth? Would he really kill her?

Of course he would try. But Uncle Androz would protect her. She had nothing to worry about, did she?

That's that, she thought. Now she would enter another phase of her life. She didn't want to, and she did feel sorrowful about it. Like everything else in life, she knew that pain vanishes in time. However, she regretted that one had to experience it in order to gain that truth.

♦

The group was waiting for Sandra, having been alerted by de Wiart that she would arrive earlier in the evening than they had expected.

However, before discussing anything, she and and Paul walked outside. "I'll help bring in your luggage," he said before she said a word. He carefully explained all that de Wiart had told them to say. However, de Wiart had also asked Paul to do something else. Paul was not to tell her anything about the late night pickup at the house until tomorrow. Let her sleep through it. "Just to be cautious," explained de Wiart.

"Let's hope that they believe you," Sandra said when Paul finished speaking.

He looked at her. "And what's been happening with you?"

She told him about her recent meeting with Walter, of course not mentioning their sexual interlude and all that had happened and had been said after that.

"Do you think that Walter believed your story?" Paul asked.

She hesitated before constructing her story. "I believe that he does, although I believe that after I left him he intended to verify it with those Nazis who had searched this house before we arrived. I did as you said, trying to convince him that I had attempted to get information for him. Of course he was disappointed, but I had the feeling that it wasn't directed at me. If he has any feeling, I believe that it will be frustration that he feels. His ego demands that he look good to Himmler and Hitler."

Paul was slightly pessimistic. "I hope that you are right. I'm glad that you didn't antagonize Walter. That would have been a mistake. But since we don't know how he feels we must act with caution about everything. Speaking of caution, I got a call from de Wiart not long ago. He wants us to leave here earlier than we had planned. Be prepared to go by about six am tomorrow morning. He wants to keep the Nazis off balance about what we are doing. De Wiart will turn over the fake Januseks to the Polish army for internment. The real ones will leave with us when we go. They want to be in Warsaw when the fighting begins. Also, de Wiart wants us to stay at a more protected place until we leave for Czestochowa and the Jasna Gora Monastery. He suggests that we stay at a small hotel in Ojcow, a small village which is about half way to Czestochowa on a very deserted road. DeWiert will ask Tomas Janusek to drive us there since he knows this area so well."

"Our plan is on target, isn't it?" There was relief in Sandra's voice when she heard Paul's words.

Paul said, "I would like to give you that assurance, GG, but I can't. When one is playing games with the Nazis in a foreign country, it sometimes is hard to know what to expect next. But congratulations on how you dealt with Walter."

Sandra saw a look of approval on Paul's face and blushed slightly. If she were asked to describe her emotions that moment, she would place guilt in a high place. As well as fear.

Paul remembered something else to tell Tomas. "De Wiart would like you to look in the garage. You now own a brand new car. Lots better than the old one, I would say. And big enough for all of us."

Everyone went to bed early since they would be up before dawn.

♦

"Put that cigarette away."

The driver of the small black pickup truck was disgusted. His regular partner for this assignment had broken his leg today and de Wiart had assigned this new man to him. "Train him," de Wiart had said. That was easier said than done, grumbled the driver. Especially on an assignment that involved split second actions. In just a few minutes--in fact it was almost ten of two and time to leave-- their truck would roll up to the Janusek house in Bielany and load the boxes in the back of the truck.

"See those containers in the back of the truck? There is gasoline in them. Can you imagine what your cigarette could start?"

"I'm sorry. You are right," mumbled the boy who was barely in his late teens.

The driver's heart softened. "Listen to me," he urged. "If you do, you will be able to survive the Nazis."

The boy nodded and the driver went on talking. "After we load the car then I'm going to turn and get back on the road again, just as if we were returning to Krakow. But we won't be. By the time we're on the road there should be a car filled with Nazis following us. They think that we'll lead them back to de Wiart's safe house in Krakow. But they are wrong."

The driver smiled.

"But what will happen?" the boy asked. He tried to cover it up, but inside he was afraid. However, he hated the Germans and wanted to help his country.

"After a few minutes of driving, I am going to make an abrupt swerve into a hidden path through the woods that I know well. I will stop the truck on the edge of a huge dropoff. When I tell you, you will get out of the truck and quickly spread the gasoline over everything in the truck, including the two dead bodies there."

Seeing the boy shiver, the driver said, "Relax. These two were bodies of homeless men we took from the local morgue. If you have spread the gasoline properly, the entire truck will explode after you and I push it over the edge. Then we will run about 50 yards to another road headed in the opposite direction. I have the keys to a car that is parked there under some heavy foliage so no one can see it. We will drive away while the Nazis are discovering that the truck containing the files they wanted is completely burned."

The driver looked at his partner. "Can you do it? Remember my life rides on your help, too."

The boy straightened up and looked at his partner. "Of course I can. We're in this together."

♦

Not that long after the crash, the police arrived and were questioning the couple who had reported the accident.

"We were returning home to Krakow after spending a few days with my wife's family," the man explained. "We heard a terrific explosion and saw the awful flames of the fire," the husband said. "Did anyone survive?"

The police captain shook his head. "It looks as if two died in the crash and the fire, although all that is left are ashes."

"Ashes," whispered a driver who had stopped to witness what happened.

His partner who was standing next to him shook his head. "We'll talk later," he said. There were too many people around who might overhear what they said. The important thing now was to get to a phone and call Schellenberg to let him know that the files were gone. "Ashes," the man said, repeating his partner's word.

"Ashes," repeated Schellenberg. All the plans he had made had gone up in flames.

He hung up the phone, completely depressed by what he had heard. Was this the end of his career or was there anything else he could do to clean up his reputation which had certainly been tarnished? He would think about that. But not now. He needed some sleep to be at his best. He took some pills out of the small container he carried in his jacket. They always helped. His last thought before closing his eyelids for a while was to wonder if all this might all be a trick that de Wiart had staged. However, he doubted that. De Wiart was smart, but was he as devious as this?

♦

Just before two am, Paul, Dave, and Harry had carried the two boxes out to the waiting car which then slowly left the grounds. Paul checked his watch. The entire operation had taken five minutes. Now back to bed for the three of them.

Paul tumbled into bed without changing his clothes. He would take a nap and shower in the morning, he decided. He was too tired now. He would have to wait until the morning anyway to have de Wiart tell them if both the real smuggling in Warsaw and the fake smuggling trick in the Krakow area had been successful.

Hardly had his head touched the pillow when he heard the slight sound of his door opening. He reached for the gun which he always placed under his pillow at night for security.

His body tensed but then relaxed when he saw the beautiful face of Sandra highlighted by the moonlight that shone into the window in his room.

"It's me," she whispered. "Don't get angry. I'm not here for what you think. It's just that I'm frightened. I keep seeing Walter's face when I close my eyes. May I curl up on your chair tonight? I promise to be good."

Paul laughed. "Even if you were at your worst, it wouldn't work. I'm too tired for anything but sleep, even when a beautiful specimen like you breaks into my room." He hit his pillow lightly. "Come here and curl up beside me. But no tricks. Right?"

"Right."

"I'll wake you up before it is time to go."

It seemed like only a moment before it was time to wake up and get ready to leave. However, when they came downstairs, a surprise awaited them.

De Wiart was sitting in the living room. When he made a V for Victory sign, everyone breathed easier. Only Paul knew the full import of that signal. It was a signal De Wiart and Paul had devised to let Paul know that both the real smuggling in Warsaw as well as the fake one in Krakow had been successful.

When they finished the coffee which Sofia Janusek had made for them and the Januseks had gushed sufficiently over their new car, de Wiart looked around at everyone and said, "Thank you for what you are doing on behalf of all those who love Poland."

Paul knew that for the usually quiet de Wiart this was indeed a very deeply felt thanks.

♦

It was not too much longer before they were on the road again. De Wiart had explained that he was uneasy about their staying here at the cabin. "Who knows what Walter might try?" he asked.

Paul agreed.

"Where I am taking you will be very safe," said de Wiart. "As well as close to Czestochowa. It will be a day of relaxation for you."

There was sufficient light as they started traveling for them to see that the area between Bielany and their destination of Ojcow covered a very picturesque section of Poland.

"Isolated," said Sofia, "but beautiful."

"A definite attraction of this area," according to Tomas, "is its castles."

Harry also knew quite a bit about this area of Poland. He said, "I still have relatives who live here, although I have never met most of them." He had visited many of the castles here. He explained that in the fourteenth century a Polish king set about fortifying the country's border by building a chain of castles between Krakow and Czestochowa. These were built on the hilltops along the ridge and, like the Great Wall of China, they formed an impossible barrier to scale by enemies.

"Why must humans fight?" Harry asked.

No one knew the answer to that.

"We will be back," promised Paul. "After the war is over. We"ll be back." But, like Sandra, Paul didn't believe that. *It's going to be a long, bad war,* he thought. He wasn't certain that the country of Poland would even exist after it had been sliced up by the greedy countries in the coming war. History would attest to the greediness of Poland's neighbors.

Tomas said, "When you return we will show you everything."

They agreed, although each wondered who would be around when such a day arrived.

Finally they reached the address in Ojcow.

De Wiart had made plans for everyone to stay with the Wajda family, a family in Ojcow that rented out rooms in their home as well as the five nearby cabins. The Wajda home was difficult to find, for it was hidden deep in the rocky land which attracts many visitors to the area. At several points Tomas stopped the car to talk about what they were seeing.

"You must expect the roads in this area to be narrow and dangerous," said Tomas. "This is an isolated area, but a beautiful one." He explained that they were now in an area of caves and rock formations. "Two major rivers meet deep inside the valley where we are standing," he said. There were no fewer than 400 large caves, grottoes, and precipices in this area known as the Polish Jura.

The car moved along slowly so they might look around them. The land was growing lusher and the air was getting more humid. "Not far from here are the area's largest caves," said Tomas. "Usually only experienced explorers will enter these caves. They are too dangerous for amateurs."

Everyone felt the quiet of the place. Paul said, "Wouldn't it be tempting to find a cave and then hide out until one day when the Nazis leave Poland?"

They all liked the idea of a hidden shelter that was safe and secure without Nazis or fascists or any groups greedy to take over the world. But that was not to be. At least, not today, for Tomas announced that they were approaching today's destination, the Wajda Guest House.

"This village was built as an inexpensive health resort in the mid-nineteenth century," Tomas told them. "Sir Androz has made arrangements for us to stay with the Wajda family. Wait in the van until I talk to the owner. Then we'll take the suitcases inside."

Everyone took a deep breath. They were one day away from their mission at Jasna Gora Monastery in Czestochowa. All of them wanted to be as optimistic as possible. And yet, each of them hid a secret fear from each other. Perhaps Paul privately summed the fear up best of all to himself by using several trite cliches that he would never use in public. Tomorrow wasn't going to be a piece of cake. Not by a long shot.

Chapter 13

A huge sign saying "Wajda Guest House" appeared just before their van maneuvered its way into the large parking lot of the guest house.

As for the Wajda Guest House, it was a site unto itself, as Paul said.

Constructed of dark brown cedar shingles, the large house had at least twenty rooms and a huge number of windows, a fact which in itself made the house light and airy. However, each of the numerous windows also featured shutters that were completely surrounded with cut-out heart shapes. The result was slightly fascinating, especially since each shutter had been painted a bright, bright, bright pink. In addition---as if such a house required any additions---each window had a flower box under it that was filled with red and white petunias, all in full bloom, mind you.

Its front door was a cheerful yellow so shiny that one could almost see one's face reflected in it. That same yellow was repeated in all of the rocking chairs that sat so invitingly on the huge wrap-around porch. And to top off a scene that really needed no topping off, the Wajda Guest House was completely surrounded by gardens of gorgeous blooming flowers that competed with each other for being the most beautiful.

In short, it was the kind of house one expects as an illustration in a children's storybook about an enchanted forest.

Everyone looked at Paul, who then looked at the house, at the woman hurrying toward them, and then at each member of his group before he spoke.

"I love it here," Paul announced with a huge smile on his face. "In fact, I may never leave."

The rest of them laughingly agreed. It was obvious that they would like to stay, too.

However, instead of a favorite character stepping out of the pages of a book, a short but very spry woman who looked to be in her mid forties quickly sprang from a side door of the house and scurried toward them. Helga Wajda introduced herself and proceeded to dole out hugs to everyone.

'Do you like our house?" she asked, although she knew already what their responses would be. "My husbnd Laszlo built it." Switching topics, she said, "Sir Androz said to tell you that he would be here later this morning."

They were going to stay in Helga's private home. "That is what Sir Androz asked for," Helga said. "For reasons of privacy," she added. Although most of the Poles referred to him as de Wiart, Paul noticed that Helga called him by his first name. As Paul discovered, they were old friends.

In no time at all, Helga had assigned a room to each of them. She said, "My four daughters will help you unpack, if you want." The rooms, all of which had the rustic country charm expected from a home decorated by Helga, also opened onto wonderful views of the many lakes and gardens on the Wajda property.

Helga soon brought steaming carafes of hot coffee to her dining table, followed by overflowing plates of various types of luscious cookies.

"This is just a snack." she cautioned. "I don't want to destroy your appetite for tonight's dinner," Helga explained. Although everyone was hungry, not having had a good breakfast this morning. Helga warned them some more. "Be sure to have a good appetite for tonight. My daughters and I are preparing a typical Polish dinner and party in your honor for tonight."

All decided that they needed a good walk before tonight if they were to be ready for that obviously huge Wajda dinner in their honor.

"My daughter Sonja is an expert guide. Would you like her to take you on a tour of the area?" Helga asked. Sonja was a sweet girl of about twelve who looked like a younger copy of her mother.

The idea pleased everyone, and in less than five minutes Sonja was leading them into the woods. Further and further she took them into an area which very soon became forest land.

"Don't worry," Sonja assured them. "I know these woods like the back of my hand."

Indeed, no one was the least bit nervous. The beauty of the woods and the wild flowers that were everywhere had taken them into a different place of contentment.

In a few minutes everyone's eyes blinked at the beauty which they now saw. In front of them was a small pool into which water flowed from over the large stones above the pond and then down into the pool. There it seemed to disappear into a grotto buried deeply inside the cave. The sounds of the water were beautiful.

Paul asked where the water flowed.

"Follow me and I'll show you," said Sonja. She led them on a path beside the pool. Finally they arrived at a stone entrance into which water was flowing.

They looked at her with curiosity, wanting to know more about this serene spot.

"We call this Wanda's Pool," said Sonja. "Wanda is a historical Polish heroine we believe lives in this grotto. We honor her by bringing her flowers whenever we visit her." Sonja placed a bouquet of the area's wild flowers across the entrance to the grotto.

"Would you like to hear her story?" she asked.

Of course they would. All sat down at the entrance to the grotto and listened while Sonja told them the story of Wanda.

King Krakus of old times had three children, two sons and a daughter. His eldest son died as a young boy at the hands of his younger cruel brother.

When he leaned of this, King Krakus banished his cruel son and named his daughter, Wanda, as queen when he died. Wanda was a beautiful queen who loved her country dearly and was loved in return by her people. Although many princes sought to marry her, she would accept none, for she was waiting for the prince who would help her to rule her kingdom wisely.

Finally a German prince named Rytigier heard about Wanda's beauty and wisdom and sent a letter to her asking for her hand in marriage. Wanda read his letter and was unhappy. The prince in his letter demanded that if he married her, her dowry should be all the land of Poland for him to rule exclusively.

Of course she would not marry him. In a firm voice she made her answer. She refused to surrender herself and her country to the Germans. Instead she would sacrifice her life for Poland.

She retired to her apartment and there prayed to God that the Poles would receive freedom from the Germans in return for the sacrifice of her life. Her prayer was granted and Wanda threw herself into a tributary of the river that at one point flowed into the cave on the Wajda property.

When her body was recovered she was buried with all honors. A plaque in her honor was raised to her memory at the cave where her body was retrieved.

When she finished Sonja pointed to the plaque that honored Wanda.

There was a hushed silence while they all thought about the similarity of the fate of Wanda to what was happening to Poland today. Again Germans were attempting to seize what wasn't theirs.

And what about Wanda? Who would be the twentieth-century version of Wanda? Who, like Wanda, could save Poland?

"Can we sit here for a few more minutes, Sonja?" asked Paul. "I want to think for a while about Wanda's story."

"Of course. When it is time to leave for dinner, I'll let you know."

Later, when they returned, they saw that Helga had closed off the dining room in her house. "It's a secret," Helga said firmly. "You will see it tonight. That reminds me. We will do some Polish folk dancing tonight in traditional Polish costumes. I have only one spare male costume and one spare female costume." Helga looked at Sandra, who tried to sound reluctant when she said that she would volunteer, even though everyone suspected that she secretly wanted to participate.

Harry spoke decisively. "We also volunteer Paul."

Helga cast a steely eye at Sandra and Paul, who both realized that this was no trivial matter.

"Be here at 6:45 so I can tell you something about the dancing that you will do. Dinner starts at 7 pm," Helga said to everyone else. Fortunately, Tomas had shared with them some basic Polish rules of courtesy on their ride here. One of them that he stressed was that they must always be on time in Poland. The Poles hold that tardiness is very rude.

Before they left to rest up for dinner Harry sought one more answer from Helga. He was curious about the pilgrims that they would see tomorrow in Czestochowa. “I understand that the roads in Poland will be filled this weekend with people traveling to Czestochowa.” Was this right, he wanted to know.

Helga nodded. “We are completely filled, in spite of the fact that we are not on the major road to Czestochowa.” The Wajda property was on an intersection of a minor road to Czestochowa, which was about twenty miles further north.

“Are these all pilgrims going to Jasna Gora?” asked Paul.

“This weekend is a religious feast day,” she reminded everyone. “Usually there are over 50,000 pilgrims per feast day who want to visit the monastery and see the portrait of the Black Madonna during our holidays. In addition to that, all Poles want to be at Czestochova this week because Sir Androz is going to be there.” She sighed. “It may be that the Nazis will overpower us when the fighting starts, but we know that Sir Androz will be fighting for us. We love him and want him to know how much we will support him in his fight against the Nazis. That’s why Poles are going to be at Czestochowa this year.”

Helga looked out the window. “See all the people walking? All of them will be searching for the Black Madonna’s help at the Jasna Gora Monastery. All those who are healthy must walk to Jasna Gora several times during their life.”

Suddenly the front door opened, and to the delight of everyone, de Wiart entered the room. When he spied his group his eyes lit up. After two straight mugs of Helga’s steaming coffee, Sir Androz looked at them and spoke. “As I told Paul, today is the day we will rest and have a good time. Tomorrow will be all business when we travel to Czestochowa.”

"We will be ready. Just tell us what to expect," replied Paul.

"Let me ask Helga if we can have a private room for a few minutes while we talk," de Wiart said.

In a few minutes everyone was sipping coffee in a quiet room. De Wiart nodded to Paul, who began. "Last night Sir Androz and I planned what will happen at Czestochowa. We think that we have covered all possibilities, but let us know what you think."

Everyone seemed relieved at that, although everyone had questions to ask later.

Paul said, "Let me remind everyone that Sir Androz's safety is our next priority. We are going to Jasna Gora to guard him while he addresses the Poles about the rightness of their desire to stand up to the Nazis when they attack Poland. Polish unity at Jasna Gora this week will show the Nazis and the entire world that evil is never triumphant, even when it appears to be."

"We do have a problem, though," said deWiart.

Everyone seemed to stiffen at that.

"All of you know Walter Schellenberg's part in all of this. Obviously he does not intend to give up his search."

Sandra's mind jumped to the worst conclusion. "Your agents tailing him lost Walter, didn't they?"

"Hold on, Sandra," de Wiart said. "I didn't have an opportunity to tell any of you that last night Walter ducked into a men's room in a restaurant and never came out. By the time we raced to a back door to the building he was long gone. However, we do know that two Nazi spies in Krakow he contacted yesterday have left for Czestochowa by car. The bad news is that both are sharpshooters."

"So we have to be ready today for Walter to appear. Right? And in a crowd that may top 50,000 pilgrims." Sandra looked very worried.

De Wiart said, "But I don't think Walter was able to recruit more than two local Nazis to back him up today. At least, that is what his last telephone call that we were able to monitor indicated. As for getting help, I don't think that he wants Berlin involved in this at all. After all, his judgment hasn't looked too good in how he has handled this situation. I am certain that Himmler, his boss, wouldn't be very happy if he knew how stupidly Walter has acted. I think this is why Walter is coming to Czestochowa. He plans on destroying someone or something at Jasna Gora in order to retrieve his reputation with the Nazis."

"Or destroy the Polish sense of purpose by stopping their demonstration," Sandra added. Although she had been surprised to learn that Walter was not giving up his chase, Sandra felt safe because of de Wiart's promise to protect her. Also, she decided that she would never tell anyone the truth about Walter's Jewish ancestors. That way she would always be safe from his anger, she thought.

"Right," said de Wiart. "But Walter is at heart a coward. I would suspect that he will turn any violence over to the two sharpshooters with him."

De Wiart said, "When we leave here, Laszlo Wajda, Helga's husband, will drive his car to Jasna Gora. We will follow him in ours, with Dave at the wheel. Laszlo knows shortcuts that we can take to avoid the crowds on the road."

Before they left to get dressed for that night's dinner, they watched Helga set up a huge table outdoors with covered sandwiches and pitches of water and juice. "As I said, it is our custom that if one can, one walks to Czestochowa and doesn't ride. This food is for the people who pass by here on the way to the services at Czestochowa," she explained. Helga had clearly outdone herself for this dinner.

Everyone assembled at the closed dining room door, waiting for the doors to open at exactly seven pm.

When the chimes began and the door opened, everyone stared at the formal buffet table that Helga had placed on the left side of the long dining room. The two tables sparkled with crystal, china, and many exquisite pieces of old Polish sterling interspersed with lovely flowers.

There were about fifteen other guests beside them at the dinner, most family members or friends of the Wajdas. After shaking each guest's hand, Helga and Laszlo, her husband, escorted each to his or her seat. When all were seated, Laszlo stood, a champagne glass in hand, and asked everyone to join him in a toast to tonight's guests of honor, de Wiart and his party.

Laszlo looked at de Wiart and said, "May I ask all of your party to stand?"

When they were standing, the host pointed his goblet at them and said, *"Na Zdrowiet,"* translated as "To your health." Everyone repeated the toast. Then various Polish liquors and wines were offered, depending on the food dish it accompanied. It is no boast to say that Polish vodka led the list of drinks called for.

Paul said, "Many say it is the world's best vodka."

"At least, all Poles do," Laszlo said with a smile.

Helga stood and spoke to the guests. "Be prepared," she said, with a look of pleasure on her face. Not only was the food wonderful, the liquor outstanding, and the conversation brilliant, but, and she emphasized this, "the dancing will be outstanding."

With that, Helga opened the sliding doors that separated another large room from the dining room. In a circle in which everyone held hands, dancers dressed in traditional Polish costumes began to move in a circular fashion to the piano music provided by one of the Wajda daughters.

The music, a Polish national folk dance, or *taniec ludowy,* grows in intensity as the dance progresses, a fact which Helga told everyone before the dance began. The men who danced were dressed in black trousers, black vest, white long-sleeved shirt, and a black hat trimmed with flowers.

The women were dressed more colorfully in long-sleeved white shirts, a very full striped skirt and vest of many bright colors, and a crown of flowers on their heads. A delicate white lace apron completed the costumes.

One of those couples, Paul and Sandra, got a special hand of applause when it was their turn to dance close to the audience.

"Paul looks a little stiff, but other than that, he's fine," said Harry. Dave whispered, "Don't the two of them look like the little couple that marches out of a cuckoo clock every hour on the hour?"

Harry couldn't resist a smile.

Good sports that they were, Sandra and Paul later attempted to keep up with the other skilled couples in a dance called the *krakowiak* before they quickly and gratefully returned to their seats. A huge burst of applause followed, the crowd insisting that the two take a bow.

"And now enjoy your meal," said Helga to her guests when the dancing was finished. "There will be more dancing if you feel up to it after the dinner."

Paul looked quickly at Sandra. He was still out of breath from the *taniec ludowy*, "I'm not up to it. In fact, I think I might need an oxygen tank."

"You'll be all right," Sandra said. She whispered into his ear. "We know what you really need."

He pushed her away with a laugh.

As for the dinner that followed, it was superb. Helga had chosen dishes that were indigenous to the various areas of Poland, with emphasis upon the area where the Wajdas lived. Accompanied by the wonderful vodka, the meal was so extensive that dinner went on for about two hours. There was so much on the tables that it was humanly impossible to even taste everything.

"But we tried," said Paul when the group discussed the dinner on the way to Czestochowa the next morning. The *kaczka pieczona z jabekami,* or roast duck with apples was loved by all, as was the *golabki,* or stuffed cabbage leaves. *Bigos,* sauerkraut and mixed meat stew was Sandra's favorite. The food went on and on.

Afterwards everyone relaxed with the wonderful Polish sweet dishes and cup after cup of Helga's coffee, which Dave had renamed as ambrosia. It was that wonderful time in the evening when conversation slows down and everyone relaxes.

Suddenly a loud cracking sound was heard, followed by the tinkle of broken glass. The men in the room got up and rushed to the living room area where the sound had come from. Like Paul, many of the men had their guns in position, anticipating that it might be the Nazis. It might be a group sent by Walter.

Helga ran into the room and saw a man entering the room from the broken window. "It's Janusz Cenar!" she exclaimed. "Why did you do this? We've been friends for thirty years. You were invited tonight. Why didn't you come?"

By now Janusz was crying. "How can you party, Helga! We all know that the Germans are going to kill us and destroy Poland. How can you laugh and sing?" Deep racking sobs now came from the heartbroken man.

The people in the room were quiet as de Wiart walked up to Janus. He embraced him tightly, allowing Janusz to cry until he had no more tears. Then de Wiart led him to a chair and got down on his knees beside him.

De Wiart held the man's hand in his as he spoke. "Tonight we laugh and dance to honor Poland, Janusz. And that is right, for we know in our hearts what may happen to Poland. In fact, we know what is going to happen to Poland very soon.

But if we believe in God, we know that there is a reason for everything. If we listen, our hearts will tell us the right thing to do. Whether we fight, whether we accept, or whatever we do, the decision must come from our hearts. As for Poland, we thank God for allowing us to live in such a wonderful place. I will always support Poland and freedom, even if it means that I must die in the attempt. But in my dying breath I will sing and celebrate my love for this country. As will you, Janusz."

Helga gently pulled Janusz from his chair. "You and I are going to lead everyone here tonight in dancing our national dance, the Polonaise."

The house shook with applause as Helga and Janusz walked to the middle of the floor and began dancing. Everyone rose to their feet and never stopped applauding until Helga and Janusz finally stopped dancing. As the couple sank to the ground in prayer, so, too, did everyone else in the room.

Janusz raised his head and spoke to de Wiart. "Of course I will go with you to Czestochowa and help celebrate Poland," he said.

"I always knew you would be there," said deWiart.

The dancing began again, more joyous than it had been before. After the evening ended, everyone pitched in and helped the Wajdas clean up. At one point Paul carried some candlesticks down the hall to the pantry. As he neared the room, he heard the sounds of someone sobbing.

It was Helga.

Paul ran to her and she clung to him. "I know that I must be brave," she sobbed. "But it is difficult."

"It certainly is," he agreed. "But everyone needs your strength. Give it to them, Helga."

"Why does God let so much evil happen?" she asked. She was quiet for a while, and then spoke with confidence in her voice. "Of course I know why. It is God's principle of plenitude. Only God knows his reasons and none of us has the right to question Him."

"Hold on to that belief and you will make it through all this." He held her in his arms until she was ready to leave.

"Thank you, Paul," she said before she returned to her world.

Paul hoped that his words about faith had helped her. Although they hadn't managed to allay his doubts, he always found it a solace to act as if he did believe.

Chapter 14

Walter was lost.

Not only did he not have any idea of where he was in this awful country, but something worse had happened to him. And it had happened only seconds ago.

With an awful blinding flash that throbbed across his forehead and pounded in every part of his body he understood that the experience of failing to find the plans had deeply affected him. Increasingly, he was losing his ability to control his thoughts or his emotions. And too, his fingers and feet were trembling uncontrollably and his head pounded so loudly that all he could do was scream. He could feel the moisture from his nose trickling down his face and wetting his lips as he mouthed his screams. His nerves were shot.

It was all the fault of that bitch Sandra and her friends. But he'd fix her. As well as her friends. He cried when he realized how they were destroying his chances of impressing Hitler. Sandra's attitude caused him to suspect that the story about jet propulsion material might be merely a red herring to make him look ridiculous. How they must be laughing at their ability to make a fool of him. The awful vision in his mind's eye of being ridiculed by Hitler caused him to black out for a few seconds. Then he got out of the car and ran to a nearby tree where he sat and sobbed. He courted the pain of his thoughts as a way of forgetting what they had done to him.

Enough, he finally told himself. He returned to his car. He must hold on, at least for a while until he got the revenge he wanted. It was that thought which had the power to bring him back from a precipice of his own. He wouldn't let himself fall apart. He would get his revenge. He would destroy those who had laughed at him and turned him into a failure.

However, he had to get to Czestochowa if he was to accomplish anything.

How carefully he had followed the map in his hand to Czestochowa, driving on the specific roads he had been instructed to use. It was a shortcut, everyone said. "Drive north from Krakow and then follow the road to Jasna Gora Monastery that goes north of it."

But it hadn't been a shortcut. All it had been was a short cut to being lost. It all began once he came to a fork in the road that was unmarked. He had became more and more lost as he tried to backtrack in this desolate area. Not one car had passed since he got lost.

He uttered a few strong German curses and then hit the steering wheel in anger. Instant pain seared through his arm. *Serves me right,* he thought. *I 'm sorry I started this.* But he did want revenge. *I do want to go to Czestochowa and make all of them suffer. But can I get there?*

The air in the car was increasingly stifling. Then, just after Walter decided to inch off the narrow road for a few minutes to pull himself together, he heard the glorious sound of a car approaching. In a minute or two a broken down, dusty jalopy had pulled up beside him. Walter pulled himself together. He must put all his plans for revenge at the back of his mind and act normal if he wanted to be helped by this driver.

"Are you all right?" asked Lech Stepic. The young driver was obviously a farmer, if the peasant clothes he wore were any indication.

Walter identified himself as Walter Cross, a tourist from Switzerland. "I'm lost," he said, looking miserable. "Someone in Krakow told me how to take a shortcut to Czestochowa, but it didn't work out. Now it will be too late to go. And I have friends waiting for me there."

"You'll make it there," Lech said with confidence. "I live about three miles north of here in Olkusz and Jasna Gora is about 20 minutes farther from there." He smiled at Walter. "I'll be glad to guide you there, if you like."

If you like?

"Fine." A relieved Walter looked at Lech's old car and made a quick decision. "How about if we leave your car and take mine for the trip? I can get mine on the way back. I am meeting some friends at the monastery today."

"Good," said Lech. "As I said, we're practically at my house. I will pick up my wife and you can leave your car at my house."

Privately Walter didn't care if he ever got the car back. He and the other two he was meeting would want to get away from the monastery as fast as they could if his scheme worked.

If it worked. Not *if,* he corrected himself. It would work.

"This is kind of you," said Walter a minute later when Lech was driving Walter's comfortable car.

"Glad to help," said Lech. "You are lucky that I had to do a last-minute errand before we left for Czestochowa. You will be company for my wife. As you found out, this is a very isolated area."

"I can attest to that!"

Lech smiled. "We have few neighbors. It is very lonely for my wife. You see, she is permanently in a wheelchair."

Walter said that he was sorry to hear that. He pretended to look compassionate.

"She once was a school teacher. And she was good at it. But she never recovered from the death of our only child, a seven-year-old girl ten years ago. After that, Maria sort of gave up hope. She's had this leg problem now for five years. The doctors here can't do anything for it. It is a chronic condition. They fear that she has only a few years to live."

Meanwhile, Walter was running the thought around in his mind that the Stepic farm might be a good hiding place for the gunmen and him after they left Jasna Gora. He would keep that in mind.

When they arrived at the Stepics, Maria was in her wheel chair sitting in front of the house, impatiently waiting to get started on the trip. As Lech had supposed, she was glad that Walter would be with them. It would be one more person to talk to.

"Sit in the back seat with me, Walter, so that we can talk," she said.

However, just before Lech started off, Walter spoke with embarrassment."I'm sorry to be a nuisance, but may I use your men's room before we leave? We may not see a gas station for a while."

"Of course," said Maria. "The door is locked, but Lech will go with you."

When both men left, Maria succumbed to temptation. In the middle of the back seat where Maria sat, she observed that Walter had carelessly thrown his coat jacket in a crumpled ball. She could see that something had fallen from a pocket onto the back seat. Half hidden by Maria's bulky wheelchair it was hard to spot. But Maria saw it. It was Walter's wallet. It took effort on her part to slide over to where the wallet was, but she managed. She picked it up and flipped through several pages. Her heart beat wildly when she read what it said. The stranger's name was Walter Schellenberg, not Walter Cross. And he was from Berlin, not Zurich, as Lech had said when he introduced the man to her. She was fairly positive that she had heard his name before in a newspaper article about some of Hitler's top men. She remembered that in the article Himmler had been mentioned as Walter's immediate superior.

The men would be returning soon. Quickly she placed the wallet back where it had been and then positioned herself as if she had been taking a short nap during their absence.

In only a minute or two they did return and they were on the road again. She realized that she must be very careful not to make the man feel that she was suspicious of him. Nazis were quick to kill anyone they thought might be a threat.

She tried to appear innocent by talking nonstop to him. Eagerly she questioned Walter about what was happening in the world, making sure, however, not to say anything disparaging about Hitler or the Nazis.

She talked so much that at one point Lech said, "Excuse Maria for talking so much, Walter. Meeting you is a big event for her."

Walter smiled at that, although he disliked having to pretend to be interested in her questions. The woman was giving him a headache.

Maria thought of something else to do that might please the man. "Are you hungry, Walter? I packed lots of lunches," she said. She told him about the old Polish custom of feeding pilgrims on the way to Jasna Gora.

Her words reminded him of how hungry he was. He gratefully accepted the bag and instantly devoured two sandwiches.

"Can you give me some information about the layout of Jasna Gora?" Walter asked. He realized that he needed to know more about the building if he were going to make plans. Lech nodded and pulled the car off the road so that he could point out to Walter the cluster of buildings that could now be seen in the distance.

"See that hill top ahead with the huge building sitting on top of it?" Lech asked. "That is the Monastery of Jasna Gora and below it is the town of Czestochowa, a town which dates from about 1382 when the Paulite Order of Monks arrived there and built the monastery. Over the years the monastery was gradually built up and fortified. On several occasions the monastery has successfully fought off attacks from neighboring countries. At the Monastery is a painting of the Virgin Mary, commonly referred to as the Black Madonna. It was presented in 1384 to the Monastery. The portrait of the Virgin Mary and her child is attributed to Luke, and the painting is said to have come from the Holy Lands. According to art critics it was in 1430 that vandals attacked the monastery and grabbed the portrait from the altar and disfigured the Virgin's face by slashing it with their swords. When the painting was restored, the dark signs of the robbers' outrage on the face of the image were kept, in memory of the barbarism that had been committed. From that moment on, the icon and Jasna Gora became symbols of religious and political liberty for the Polish people."

It was difficult for Walter to keep a straight face at what Lech was saying. The Poles were going to need more than a monastery and a painting to save them from us, Walter thought.

Lech continued.

`"The town below the Monastery grew as a center for the pilgrims who began visiting the monastery to see the painting for its miraculous restorative powers. In 1717 Poland crowned the Black Madonna painting as the 'Queen of Poland.' "

Walter interrupted. It was details about the monastery that he needed, not history. "How is the monastery laid out?" he asked. "Can you tell me that?"

"Of course," said Lech. "Any Polish schoolboy can tell you that. I'll give you an overview. Interrupt me if you have a question." He took out a piece of paper and made a drawing of the monastery to illustrate what he was saying. He said, "There are four main gates for entrance to the Cathedral and to the Chapel of the Holy Virgin May where the Black Madonna is displayed. These are just to the right of the outdoor information center outside. Follow the crowds as they enter for they will lead you to the ornate Chapel of the Holy Virgin Mary. After that, visitors are free to tour the Monastery at will. Remember that today a Memorial Mass will be held outdoors in the square where pilgrims enter the Monastery. The Mass will be followed by an address outdoors by de Wiart. Then the Archbishop, Sir Androz, and all the prominent civil and religious guests sitting on the outdoor stage will return to the Cathedral. The procession will end back at the Chapel of the Holy Virgin where it began."

Lech looked solemnly at Walter. "For six decades Poland's enemies have attempted to destroy Jasna Gora. The Black Madonna will always protect Poland, even against the Nazis."

We'll see about that, was what Walter was thinking. However, all he said was, "Thank you. That gives me a good idea of the scope of the building. And at what time does the Memorial Mass begin today?"

"I believe at 2:45, but you better check that out."

As Lech had promised, it wasn't much longer before they arrived at the Monastery's grounds. Because they were early, Lech found a good parking spot for handicapped pilgrims in the large lot reserved for cars. He turned off the motor and then held the car keys out to Walter.

"No, you hold onto them," Walter told him. "What time do you want to leave the Monastery today? I'll meet you here at the car." Walter was beginning to believe that going home with the Stepics might be the safest way to escape the Monastery. Things seem to be going well, he thought. This morning before he started on the journey he had cut his hair himself and had bought a pair of metal rim glasses to wear. He probably wouldn't be recognized, although he wouldn't stay in public places if he could avoid it. He would also try to steal someone's hat, if he could.

The opportunity to drive a new car like Walter's was fine with Lech. The three of them said that they would meet at the car at six pm. "We need to take some time to have a cup of coffee and relax before we meet you, particularly Maria," said Lech. "This is a long day for her."

"After one pm the painting of the Black Madonna is available for all to see on the hour," Lech explained. "Maria and I will tour the entire monastery and then be in the courtyard when Sir de Wiart begins to talk to the group at 3:15 pm. After that the three of us will meet at your car at about six pm, give or take a few minutes."

Walter was startled to hear the number of pilgrims de Wiart would be speaking to. What a coup it would be if he could eliminate such an important symbol of Polish resistance to the Nazis. He looked at his watch. He and the sharpshooters would meet at the spot they had already designated at 12:30 to plan what they were going to do today. Walter was excited at the thought.

Lech noticed that the parking area was becoming filled. "Maria should get out of the car soon so that we can avoid the crowds," he said.

"Can I help you lift her out of the car?" asked Walter.

"No," Maria said quickly. "I'll stay in the car and eat my lunch here before we start touring," she said. "But thanks, Walter."

"Then I'll see you both here later," Walter said.

Maria pretended to be talking to Lech while Walter took his jacket out of the back seat. Out of the corner of her eye she heard him curse and then she saw him frantically search the area around his jacket. With obvious relief he scooped up his wallet when he finally saw it lying on the floor. Maria held her breath. What would he think? She kept on talking to Lech in order to look as casual as she could. She breathed more easily when she saw Walter put his wallet away. He was not suspicious at all.

"See you later," he said as he left.

Maria waved goodbye to him. However, when she saw that Walter was far enough away not to hear, she called Lech, asking that he sit beside her in the back of the car for a few minutes. "Quickly," she said.

Rapidly she told him about the contents of the wallet. Lech was stunned. "Walter is a Nazi?" he kept repeating.

"And an important one. He must want to destroy something here. Did you notice how he questioned you about the Cathedral? I'm certain that he has some awful thing planned. Here's what we must do."

Lech was to see if he could pick up Walter's trail after he left them. "But don't let him see you. See where he goes, if you can. But don't go any further than that. Next, go to the office of the Jasna Gora security office and ask to see de Wiart immediately. Explain the story and bring him back here to me as soon as possible."

Her intuition told Maria that she was right to be suspicious of this man she and her husband had befriended. She hoped that she could be in time to foil any plot he might have. She prayed to the Black Madonna for help. It wasn't the first time that Poland had been threatened by its enemies. And it probably wouldn't be the last time, she told herself sadly.

Chapter 15

Within ten minutes Paul and the others had received Lech's message. De Wiart wasn't available, having left for a few minutes to tour some security measures that had been enacted for today.

"Can you provide a room where we can talk to Maria privately about Schellenberg?" Paul asked the security chief at Jasna Gora. "I don't want any of our group to be seen by Walter or his men. And also, don't move the Stepic car. I don't want Walter suspicious about anything."

By the time Maria was brought to them Sir Androz had also returned to listen to what she had to say. She told them everything that she remembered about Walter. "Once I realized that he was a Nazi, I listened carefully to what he said so that I could repeat it to you. We do know where Walter will be after the program." She explained the arrangements that she and her husband had made with him.

"Did you get any indication of where Walter and his two allies were going to meet when he left you?" asked Sandra.

Maria shook her head. "That was why I asked Lech to follow Walter to see where he was headed."

Everyone looked at Lech hopefully. "I tried but I couldn't find Walter after I left Maria. I wish I could tell you more than that," Lech said. "But I can't. He rushed away as if he didn't want to be followed."

Paul looked at his watch. "It is noon. Walter told Maria that he was meeting his friends at 12:30 We don't know where that meeting is to be. For now I suggest that we break up into groups of two and search those parts of the Monastery that Walter questioned Lech about. The goal for now is to find them without their being aware that we are on to them. Once we know where they are we'll use all the security people that Sir Androz brought with him today to catch Walter."

He looked at Sir Androz. "Will you follow a suggestion from me if I offer it?"

"Possibly," he said cautiously. The laughter from the group broke the tension.

Paul said, "I want you to stay here in this room. With Maria. Let us do the search. That's an order. You are an icon of belief for the Polish today. I want you safe. All right?"

Sir Androz shook his head reluctantly.

"And Sandra, put a scarf or something around your hair to hide it. Walter knows you well. You could spoil everything if he recognizes you."

"Even my own father won't recognize me when I'm finished," she promised.

Lech stepped forward rather nervously. "May I join you? I am an expert shot and I will join the resistance when Hitler marches in. Just give me a gun. Plus, I can help identify Schellenberg. I saw him up close today." He shuddered. "I couldn't forget that Nazi's face."

"Let him help," asked Maria. Her eyes sparkled with excitement and love. "He is an excellent shot and a Polish patriot."

"Fine. You have just become one of us, Lech. Let's get organized." Paul used a diagram of Josna Gora supplied by the director of security to assign the groups to specific areas of the Monastery. He divided the squarish structure into four parts and assigned people to each section. Each group was told to be back by 1:30, if possible.

"Try not to look as if you are conducting a search," Paul advised. "And act as if you are a visitor by lingering over certain paintings or areas that you admire. But search every inch," he added.

He held up a photo of Schellenberg and a rough sketch of the man provided by Lech. "We think that he will have altered his appearance by now. However, this will be a guide for you." Paul distributed copies to everyone. "If you do see this man, do not attempt to take him in custody. Let us know immediately. We do not want any innocent pilgrims taken as hostages. Now go see if you can find Schellenberg and his men!" he said.

Paul appreciated the few quiet moments of reflection he had after the others left. He sat in a chair near the entrance to the Chapel of the Virgin, the chapel that housed the Black Madonna. At the entrance he saw a wrapped package sitting behind the entrance fence. That must be the copy of the Black Madonna that his group would be taking back to England. They had thought that Schellenberg might believe it held the plans for jet propulsion. It was possible that he had not yet seen it.

The scent of the church seemed to intensify for Paul. It had to be the scent of incense, but he found it overlaid with another smell, which as a child he had called the "church smell," that indefinable affirmation of God's presence that seemed to pervade every church he had ever entered, enforcing his belief that what religion provided best was the smell of God 's presence, not its theology, nor its dogma. What one received, whether from a church, a synagogue, a mosque, or a meeting house, was the overwhelming scent of God. A lapsed Christian, he was aware that his nose no longer had much ability to pick up the smell. Why, he wondered, had he allowed that to happen?

At his back he began to hear the sound of footsteps and hushed voices, but voices nonetheless.

On one side of the Chapel was a huge candle holder holding row after row of burned out candles. Quickly he pulled out a coin from his pocket and dropped it in the box next to the candle holder. Picking up a match from a nearby box he struck it and held it to the wick of a candle he selected from a box on the table. When it lit, he screwed the candle into a socket, where it glowed with a strong light. From his chair he gazed at the light, allowing its presence to take him deep into himself.

Chapter 16

It was no problem for Walter.

He easily found the dark blue car with the dented right and left fenders that he was looking for on the north side of the vast parking lot at Jasna Gora. After all, how many cars met that description?

He knocked once on the front passenger door.

"You're late," said one of the two men sitting inside the car.

"I'm lucky to be here," Walter said angrily. "And that's no business of yours, anyway. You report to me, remember? I only wish that I had some of my Berlin agents here instead of a reject like you."

The man reacted angrily to Walter's words. "Let's get one thing straight. We get paid for this job. Right? Because if we don't, I don't play."

Walter looked at him intently. His right arm rose quickly and he shot the man between the eyes. The silencer on the gun made the sound minimal.

"And you?" Walter moved his gun to the head of the other man. That man shifted nervously in his seat.

"I'm with you," the man said quickly. "I have no problems with how the Nazis have treated me. I expect my reward when the Nazi troops hit Poland."

"Good."

The man pointed to the body. "Before you arrived, this idiot and I examined the Monastery, looking for the best place for a person to hide so that he could kill someone within the Monastery and yet have a chance of escaping."

"Excellent. Tell me what you suggest."

Quickly the gunman explained his idea, as well as what they needed to do in order to execute it. The plan was simple and clean, Walter decided. It had a good chance of working. Now to get ready for it.

"Leave the body here in the car until it is dark tonight. It is too light right now to move it," Walter said.

Meanwhile, Paul had given strict orders that Maria was not to leave the director of security's office. "Remember that Walter knows what you look like, Maria. If he sees you he might go on alert. We would never be able to find him in this crowd."

However, Maria convinced him to give her five minutes outside the director's office. "May I visit the camera and film shop next door?" asked Maria. "I forgot my camera. I want to take pictures so that I will be able to remember Jasna Gora." It may be a long time before I see it again after today, she thought sadly.

Perhaps never, thought Paul. "But make it fast," he said, insisting that one of de Wiart's men go with her. "Five minutes only, Maria," he warned.

There was a long line of customers at the store when she arrived. Maria waited patiently to pay for the camera she had picked out. She tried not to lose her temper, although it was difficult because the man in front of her kept asking questions about how to use the camera he had just purchased. She looked at the tall, blond haired man in irritation. Obviously in his twenties, he should know more about a camera than he did. *Unbelievable,* thought Maria. He even asked the clerk to load the camera for him.

But finally he ran out of questions and left. Maria and her companion made it back to the safety director's office within the five-minute framework of time which Paul had given her.

♦

When everyone returned from their scouting expedition of the Monastery Paul grilled them. “Did you see any sign of Walter or two men acting suspiciously?” he asked.

No one had.

Harry said, “But I did get a feel for how difficult it is going to be to protect ourselves today here at the monastery. It’s like a labyrinth of small and large rooms where a killer could hide himself without our knowing it. My suggestion is that we limit our appearances.”

“What do you mean?” asked Sandra.

“Harry is right,” said Dave. “None of us, including de Wiart, should tour the Monastery today. There is just no way that we can guarantee total security. All we can do, and we can do it well, is to protect de Wiart when he addresses the pilgrims outside the monastery at 3:15 pm. I don’t know how everyone else feels, but I am convinced that de Wiart is Walter’s major target. To eliminate him would be to kill the heart of Polish resistance to the Nazis. That means that we will surround him entirely when he walks out of the monastery to the outdoor podium, we will surround him entirely while he sits on the stage, we will surround him around the podium while he speaks, and then we will surround him when he exits the speaking area. At that point, our secure car will be parked close to the nearest and safest exit from the Monastery.”

Paul turned to Harry and Dave. “You two will check with the Monastery’s security director to find out which exit we should use use. You also will personally check out the exit. After de Wiart speaks we will whisk him and us out of here to the airplane that will be waiting for us.”

It was obvious from the expression on his face that de Wiart wasn’t too happy about Harry’s plan. He wondered aloud if he really needed such heavy security.

Paul looked at him and spoke very firmly. "We're right about this. We must be extra careful today. We have no idea of how many assassins Walter has in place or what they look like."

Paul turned to Dave. "I want you to make a diagram of the outdoor speaking area. Assign specific people to totally surround De Wiart during the times I mentioned."

Paul said to de Wiart, "How many men can you assign to me for this detail?"

De Wiart thought for a few seconds and then pulled a sheet from his pocket and showed it to Paul. He said, "This is a complete list of all of the Polish resistance members here at the Monastery. I can give you thirty additional men."

"Thirty plus our original group will be sufficient," Paul said. He returned the list to de Wiart. "Ask them to report immediately to Dave in this room. He will give each man a schedule and tell him what his job is."

"We also need to be able to communicate with each other," Paul said. "Any suggestions?"

Sandra looked at the man de Wiart had appointed to guard Maria and said, "Jan Sowinski will always be in this room. Appoint Jan as coordinator and give him a list of where everyone is. Assign two other men as runners for Jan so that he can get messages."

"Good plan," said Paul. He looked at his watch again. "We don't have much time. I want everything in order by 2:20 at the latest." He sighed. "One thing more. Everyone is to carry a pistol and a knife. Remember that we play for keeps. I will feed everyone information as I receive it. The wrapped copy of the painting will sit outside the Chapel of the Virgin. Watch to see if someone tries to take it."

By now all the plans had been made. Hopefully, they would work.

"Hopefully," Maria said to herself. Her thoughts idly sifted through today's events. She knew what Walter looked like, but what about those "friends" of his? Walter had seemed rather cowardly to her. She was certain that he would rely on the friends to do the assassination. *Come on, Maria, think,* she told herself. If she wanted to assassinate someone in a large crowd, how would she get close enough to her victim to do it?

Suddenly she thought of several ways it could be done.

Oh, my God, she thought. *It could be done.*

She thought back on the man in front of her at the camera shop next door. Why not someone posing as a photographer? How easy it would be to get close enough to the victim if you were thought to be a commercial photographer working at his or her job.

She said, "Jan, ask the press officer for the monastery if any press passes were issued for a photographer today. Better still, ask the press officer to stop here for a moment."

Soon Jan's runner had returned with a young nun in tow.

Maria quickly described the man who had held up the line at the camera store today. "All because he couldn't take a picture," said Maria. What if he was only pretending to be a photographer?

The nun in charge of press passes hadn't been approached by anyone with that description asking for a press pass. "However, we do provide location privileges for authorized photographers," she said. "But no one applied today. We have a professional agency responsible for picture taking today. But their photographers have been cleared by us since we always use the same photographers. However, I must admit that I have employees here at the Monastery who out of a kind heart have from time to time allowed non-press pass people with cameras to stand in the front areas with commercial photographers."

Maria thanked the nun. She looked at Jan and then at her watch. There were exactly 29 minutes until 2 pm. "Ask Paul or Sandra to come here, please, Jan. Tell them that I am sorry to call them, but what I have to say is important." Could anyone stop Schellenberg? Maria wasn't certain that it could be done with all the people at the Monastery today.

But she knew that everyone was going to try.

Chapter 17

Sandra was right behind Paul when they rushed into the room to hear what Maria wanted to tell them.

She was anxious to hear what Maria had to say, even though she was torn about what she wanted to hear from Maria. On one hand she hoped that Maria knew something that would allow them to catch, or even better, kill Walter and any accomplices he had with him. That would be in everyone's best interest, including hers, for then there would be no Walter around to implicate her in any of this. And yet on the other hand, she still felt an emotion for Walter. She would give anything she had to spend life with Walter. *Too late.* T*hat's too dangerous, you idiot,* she told herself. She had to control that feeling. She shuddered when she thought about how often similar throbs had gotten her into trouble.

"I have something important to tell you," Maria said to the group. "Anyone can be wrong, and if I am, I apologize. But here is what I believe is the situation."

She finished telling them about her incident with the customer at the camera store. "In addition to not knowing one end of a camera from the other, there was something wrong about his clothing. I didn't get a good look at him, but I did get an impression about him. I saw that he was wearing a heavy gold ring which had been turned so that the stone was not visible. I remember staring at his neck. He was also wearing a turtle neck sweater whose collar was pulled up high to camouflage something round his neck. Here's what I think. Our assassin is smart. To get close enough to de Wiart he realizes that he has to do something or be someone who could request a preferred place at the event. Who would receive more preferment at a religious ceremony than a priest? Especially if that priest asked to be close to the speaker so that he might take pictures."

"Do you have any proof of this, Maria?" Paul asked. It was obvious that he was working at keeping any impatience out of his voice, but time was short, as a quick look at his watch was confirming.

She shook her head. "Only my intuition—and some logic in a belief that our shooter has to be close if he wants his shot to be effective. I do have an idea. May I join the group protecting Sir Adroz? That way I'll be able to want to test out my theory."

Sandra was relieved to hear the tentativeness in Maria's voice. Maria really had no direct information to offer about Walter. With that realization Sandra's spirits rose. Perhaps everything had already worked itself out. Walter might have decided that nothing would be settled. He might already have left Czestochowa. Oh, if only that were the case!

"Give Maria a chance. She deserves that," Sandra said, looking at Paul. She wanted to sound as though she believed Maria had a point. But that wasn't completely why she was saying what she did. It was simply that if push came to shove and Walter was proven to be behind this effort to seize the war materials, or to harm de Wiart, Sandra wanted to keep Walter from involving her in any of this.

Paul shook his head, "I can't do that, Sandra. Neither you nor Maria can be in the processional or on the outdoor stage, either. Walter might see you. All I can do is allow the two of you to be in a small room near the Chapel of the Virgin. There is a window in the room so that you can look out and see if you can locate Walter as the processional moves to the outdoor stage. However, when the outdoor program is over and de Wiart moves inside, that is a different story. We can surround and protect everyone, including you and Maria, by using the extra men that de Wiart says he will give me. As far as I am concerned, I see no problem if the two of you join the public group near the Chapel of the Virgin when the processional returns there. However, I want the two of you to be disguised even then so that Walter doesn't see you while you are looking for him. Is that understood? "

He looked so stern that they both felt obligated to say that they would follow his rules. However, Sandra whispered to Maria. "I'll make certain that I am always near you. If you need me, just raise your hand and point at what you want me to see. Good luck!"

Sandra hoped that she had covered all bases. At least, she couldn't think of anything else that needed to be done. She had a gun. And she would use it, she vowed to herself.

Time was growing short.

Paul reminded everyone that promptly at 2:20 pm the procession of those who would be on the outdoor stage would meet inside at the Black Madonna Chapel. "From there Monsignor Welenska and de Wiart will lead the procession from inside Jasna Gora to the monastery's outdoor stage."

So that they might gauge their time, Paul itemized the order of the processional for them. "Following the Monsignor and de Wiart will be a group composed of leading religious and governmental figures, followed by a procession of priests and nuns in attendance at today's services. A procession of handicapped pilgrims who wished to be on the stage will be last to enter. De Wiart's security guards will completely surround him and will be stationed at regular spots among the participants on stage and around the audience below. After the mass led by Monsignor Welenska, de Wiart will then speak to the masses of pilgrims below him."

"What happens when he finishes?" Maria asked.

"Those sitting on the stage reverse their previous path to the stage by processing to the Black Madonna Chapel inside the monastery," Paul said. "That ends the services for the day. All the pilgrims then decide what they want to do for the rest of the day. If everything goes as it should, you, Lech, and I will then go to the Stepic car. Schellenberg agreed to meet the Stepics there after the stage ceremonies. Meanwhile, we will have a car as close as possible to the Monastery exit that Harry and Dave have decided to use so that we can leave the monastery area quickly."

"Maria and I will hunt for Schellenberg among the groups of priests who are inside at the Madonna Chapel when the procession ends." Sandra looked at Paul. "I have a feeling that those confused moments might be an opportune time for someone to try to get at de Wiart."

"You may be right. Fortunately the extra security guards that de Wiart is posting will solve the problem of security for everyone," said Paul.

Sandra steeled herself for what was to come. She was nagged by a guilty hope that she might keep Paul from ever learning how she had not followed his instructions for how to act during her last meeting with Walter. How could she tell him that his directions to her had been countermanded by de Wiart? But nothing was going to go wrong today, she kept telling herself. What was going to happen would happen the way de Wiart wanted it to happen. And too, Walter and the supposed assassin were probably long since gone. She was certain of that. Walter was too shrewd to allow himself to be caught in a trap. And so was she. After all, she was Max's daughter, wasn't she?

Chapter 18

"When Lech returns he'll join the two of you here," Paul said.

He personally had led the two women to the small room. "You will be safe here. This is the beginning of the line for guests who walk from the Chapel of the Miraculous Image—the official name for the room where the Black Madonna painting is displayed--to the open air square in front of the Jasna Gora Monastery."

"I don't want Walter or his men to spot you," Paul repeated several times as if he felt guilty for requiring them to stay in the room. "You will be able to look out some small windows while the lines are forming. No one will see you but you can see well from here."

Both Maria and Sandra reluctantly agreed. As much as they would prefer to be out among the public, neither believed that the walk to the stage was going to be the crucial part of this day. Maria believed that it would be when the stage groups returned to the area around the Chapel when the outdoor program was over. That would be when the danger would begin. Any killers would welcome the confusion created by the climax of such an important occasion as this was for Poland.

"We don't have to stay in this room while everyone is processing back here, do we?" asked Sandra. "It wouldn't make sense."

"No," Paul agreed. "Just before the program on the stage outside ends, men will escort you from this room so that as a group you can then line the left and right aisles of those returning from the stage to this area. De Wiart has promised extra men to protect you."

Maria said, "Sandra and I will bury ourselves in the crowds of pilgrims waiting here who want a final look at de Wiart when he returns. That way we won't look obvious. No one will notice us, but we'll be able to look carefully at who is coming. If either of us sees anyone suspicious, we will make a signal to the men surrounding us to seize the person, or even the persons."

Paul nodded. "Don't try to be a hero and think that you can capture Schellenberg or his allies," he warned. "We have plenty of de Wiart's men here to help us. Is that clear?" He looked at each woman with that message obvious in his eyes.

They nodded.

"Then I'll see you after everything is over. Good luck." He kissed each on the cheek.

♦

After he left the two women realized that a long wait was in store for them until the program was over. Nervous, they could make the time go faster and get over their jittery feelings by talking about their roles today, suggested Maria.

"If I see a familiar face, I'll raise my arm once. That should be enough to alert our guards," said Maria. The two women did a practice run so that Sandra knew exactly how Maria would alert everyone. They also decided to cover Maria's wheel chair with a blanket so that it was less obvious to anyone.

"The crowds will be so heavy that Walter or his men will have trouble identifying us," said Sandra, who had also tied a scarf tightly around her head but not tight enough to ruin her hairdo. "No one will recognize me now," she laughed.

However, Maria still fretted. "It's those beautiful eyes of yours," she said to Sandra. "They stand out like a beacon."

Sandra thought about that and pulled a pair of reading glasses from her purse.

"Better?" she asked.

"Somewhat," said Lech, who had just joined them.

"You are too beautiful," said Maria. "But we can't change that."

"Let's see what we can from the windows," Maria suggested to Sandra when they began to hear the sounds of those stage guests who were assembling near the entrance to the Chapel of the Miraculous Image in order to march to the huge upper stage of the outdoor grounds. This upper stage, sitting high above the open grounds, had been transformed so that a memorial mass could be held there by Cardinal Wilenska. On the left and the right side seats had been reserved for the priests and nuns as well as for prominent government invitees for the day.

Fifty yards in front of all this was a lectern from which de Wiart would speak to the audience below the upper stage after the mass had been celebrated. More than anything else, Maria and Sandra regretted that they would not hear what de Wiart had to say to the Polish people. However, they agreed with Paul that exposing themselves on the stage would have been very dangerous.

By now those who would be processing onto the outdoor stage had begun to walk. Their march began to the accompaniment of some magnificent music coming from the monastery organ.

Sandra bent over to speak to Maria. "Whatever happens, Maria, I thank you for all you are doing to keep my uncle safe."

Maria smiled. "He means a great deal to us. He is very much the soul of Poland. He is the living embodiment of the value of commitment and the courage to do the right thing despite any odds."

There was little to do while they waited.

Except to pray, thought Sandra.

Although they were too far from the stage to hear any words distinctly, some of the sounds of the mass could be heard. Actually, enough of it came through to bring tears to the eyes of the two women. This place, this Poland, what was soon going to happen to it?

Could there be a resolution of the conflict so that war was averted? wondered Sandra. Should she pray for that? She would, but at the same time she would ask that God's will be accomplished. That prayer always provided more solace to her. As for Sandra there was one more request she made. Perhaps the averting of war might allow Walter and her to once again be together.

It hardly seemed any time at all until a tumultuous roar was heard in the small room where the women were. It got louder and louder, as if threatening that it would never end.

"I bet that Uncle Androz is being introduced," Sandra said, her eyes sparkling.

Maria nodded. "I wish that we could hear his words."

"But we already know them, don't we?"

"Right." They would never forget de Wiart's words at the Wajda dinner.

During the next forty minutes they heard frequent loud bursts of applause. Then came the crescendo. "Sir Androz must be finishing up," said Maria.

With that came a light knock at their door. The women were frightened at first. Had Walter seen them?

However, it was de Wiart's guards. "We think it might be a good idea to take your places now," one man said to the two of them. "The procession from the stage will be starting any moment."

It was time.

Although Maria and Sandra felt a sudden fear, their confidence soon returned. They were ready. In fact, Sandra was more than ready. Once this afternoon was over, she would be free to start a new life. She was certain of that, although she knew how much she would miss Walter. But she would adjust.

She had learned to be an expert at adjusting.

De Wiart's men had a good idea about Maria's wheelchair. They had brought with them a crate that was at least two foot high and wide enough and strong enough to hold the wheelchair. When they set it up Maria was able to see over many heads so that she might know who was coming. Sandra stood a row behind Maria. Everyone waited for the groups to enter the Outer Chapel from the stage.

Maria had a good seat from which to view the proceedings. She looked around her and around Sandra to find the men de Wiart had assigned to guard them. She wanted to thank them for their help. However, she couldn't find them. She was certain that they were there, though. She would look for them later if she remembered.

The procession began.

First, an honor guard of government and religious flags appeared. There was an electricity in the air which was almost palpable, Sandra thought, as the march into the Chapel began.

Now it was time for the Cardinal and then de Wiart to walk past Maria and Sandra. However, the paths of the two men were partially blocked by the crowds of people kneeling on the ground in front of them at the Chapel in order to show their love for the Cardinal and de Wiart. The procession slowed down to a slow pace.

Cardinal Wilenska and de Wiart had just managed to reach the entrance to the room housing the Black Madonna painting when it happened.

Maria's arm had shot into the air.

At that signal Sandra saw that one of the priests who had been in the Inner Chapel and who was down on his knees in front of de Wiart had risen. She also saw the gun that he was raising in order to shoot de Wiart.

That priest fell when Sandra's gun rang out like an explosion. At the same time, another priest next to the one Sandra had shot pulled a knife from under his robe and ran to Sandra. He began to gouge slices in Sandra's face in an almost ritualistic rhythmic pattern.

The priest was Walter. He had posed as a priest in order to get to her as well as to de Wiart.

Why me? she wanted to call out. *Why did you do this to me?*

She thought about that. Hadn't her life showed her the truth? Wasn't she living proof that those who love us or those whom we love can be those who cause us the most pain? *Aren't they often our executioners? S*he felt her tears begin when she saw the half-crazed expression on Walter's face as he made each new cut.

A blinding certainty hit her. She was going to die. She realized with certainty that this was how death came. All she had to do was let go and accept it.

In agony Sandra reached for Walter in an attempt to save herself. She flung herself on him so that she might seize the knife he wielded. While she tried, Walter continued with his knife, his face filling with pleasure and hate with each new slash he made. Unable to take the knife from him, instead she kneed him. The pain surprised him enough so that she could knock the knife out of his hands. Although she could not see for the blood that covered her face, she searched the floor for his knife. However he found it first. With a triumphant smile he slashed again and again at her face, sometimes slicing the flesh but often slashing only the air in his fury. Frustration and failure had exploded within him to create the satisfying fury of an attack that may have lasted only seconds, but for Sandra, these were seconds that felt like hours.

Only seconds after Walter's attack began, Sandra heard and felt a second explosion. Suddenly bodies were leaping through the air, furiously attempting to pull Walter away from her and to stop his stabbings.

She found herself screaming wildly. The pain had become unbearable. Suddenly from somewhere she heard a voice calling out to her. She turned toward the voice blindly. De Wiart's open arms enveloped her while her body shook with sobs. His familiar touch succeeded in lessening her terror. Just as her father had always told her, "It's all right, Sasha. It's all right," whenever she needed consolation, it was now de Wiart's voice that she heard saying the same words to her.

"It is not all right," she cried to de Wiart. "It never is for Sasha." With that her mind took her back into her past. With a rush she realized that she could recall the weather of that day, the smell of the crops drying in the sun, the music of the swaying trees, as well as the smell of their fingers that day when her brother had sold tickets to her rape.

"It is not all right," she screamed now to de Wiart as she held onto him. "Please love me. I did the right thing."

Her eyes watched Walter running from the building just before she lost consciousness. Now she was removed from evil to be a free spirit looking down at herself from the beautiful blue sky. It was a moment of understanding for her, a time when everything was a different reality and when human rules no longer applied. It was a moment of peace for her before a nothingness set in and captured her, using its power to fuse into one blackness all the realities of the human past, the present, and the future.

♦

Paul reached the scene in seconds and saw what Walter had done to Sandra. He made some quick decisions.

"Get a doctor here as soon as possible," he called out. Directing two men to Sandra's side he told them to squeeze her major facial gashes together until the doctor arrived. "Let her stay unconscious until the doctor is here." That would keep the pain away. For a while, Paul thought grimly.

"The assassin Sandra shot is dead," Harry told him.

"Good." Paul yelled, "Which direction did Walter take?"

The other man, now definitely identified by Maria as Walter, had turned to the left when he ran out of the room, spectators told Paul. He realized that Walter was looking for a door that would take him outside to the crowds of people here today. Once he did that, Paul knew that it would be next to impossible to find him.

"You two get the guards to close off as many gates as possible. I want the Lubomirskis Gate, the Queen of Poland Gate, and the Jagiellonian Gate closed. Also tell the officials to get all the public out of the Monastery grounds as soon as they can without frightening everyone," Paul yelled to Harry and David as they all ran in pursuit of Walter.

Although there probably were a lot of exits from the buildings in the Monastery, Paul knew of only the major ones. These were at *Bastion Lubomirskich,* or the Arsenal, the *Skarbiec*, or the Treasure, and the other an exit not far from the Bell Tower. Paul would try all of them, with the Room of the Treasure first.

Paul entered the *Skarbiec* with his gun drawn. The room, one that contains all the votive treasures which Jasna Gorna has received from pilgrims through the years, is long and narrow, making it easy for him to see that it harbored no one.

Paul would explore the *Bastion Lubomirskich* next.

He felt a strange feeling as he walked to the *Bastion Lubomirskich,* the parapet wall that had once fortified the Monastery from invaders. It was still performing the same task today. Paul explored the entire area, peering down from the wall in this open parapet wall to the ground below. It was too high for anyone to jump from. That would be instant death, Paul decided.

But where was Walter?

It was then that Paul heard the slight sound that a door always makes when it is closed slowly.

The sound had come from the Bell Tower. Walter had just entered the Bell Tower.

Paul was puzzled. Where had Walter hidden while Paul searched the *Bastion Lubomirkisch?* To get to the Bell Tower Walter would have had to cross the open parapet and thus would certainly have been seen by Paul. Paul looked around, puzzled. But then he realized what Walter had done. There was a public telephone booth at the end of one side of the *Bastion.*

Paul berated himself for being so slow. Walter had hidden himself in the bottom of the telephone booth, only making a run for freedom and the Bell Tower when Paul had walked in the opposite direction.

But hold on.

Paul knew that the Bell Tower had only one exit, and that was through the door where Paul was standing. How did Walter ever hope to get out of that trap?

When he thought about that question he realized that he knew what Walter would do next.

Paul held his gun in front of him and slowly turned the knob of the door, jumping to the side as he did it. A spurt of bullets followed, striking the spot in front of the door where Paul would have been if he had not suspected that Walter was standing next to the door, waiting to shoot him.

He heard Walter scrambling up the steps of the Tower.

"Don't tire yourself out too much," Paul said in a loud voice so that Walter could hear what he was saying. "There are no other doors in the Tower. But there are two windows, one on the second floor, and one on the sixth. Unless you want to commit suicide, you might consider coming down here."

"Come up and get me," yelled Walter.

"Of course I won't. Surrender to me now or to the guards I will post at this door."

He heard the sound of steps coming down. But Walter wasn't finished yet. Paul knew that.

"I'm here," Walter said. "Open the door."

Paul did. He and Walter stared at each other.

"Can you shoot while you are looking at me? Sounds cowardly to me," taunted Walter.

"Then suppose both of us play fairly. If you throw your gun across the roof, I will, too," answered Paul. "I want an opportunity to beat the hell out of you."

Walter looked suspiciously at Paul, trying to calculate what type of chance he had to come out of this alive without a gun. But what if Paul was stupid enough to fight it out? It was a chance. He couldn't see any other route that was better.

"At the count of three, throw the gun down," said Paul

Walter's gun bounced when he dropped it. Paul also threw his down at the same second.

"Okay, you bastard. Let's see what you can do," said Paul.

As soon as he could, Walter gouged Paul's eye. "Did you think I would play fair?" laughed Walter. "Of course not." He kicked Paul so hard that Paul went down on one knee in pain and doubled over. Walter went in for the kill, bending over so that he could punch Paul in the head.

It was then that Paul landed a left to Walter's head that was so hard that Walter saw stars for a few seconds.

Paul lifted his foot and slammed it into Walter's stomach. "Whatever made you think that I would play fair?" he said. He scrambled to the two guns and picked them up. "Go ahead, Walter, make a break for it."

"So you can shoot me in the back?"

"Well, if you don't like that, how about in the face?" Paul aimed as precisely as if he were at target practice. He shot Walter between the eyes.

"Bull's eye," he said.

♦

"De Wiart has plans for Walter's body," he told Dave and Harry a few minutes later when they arrived. "Ask me about it, but later today." He wanted to get back to Sandra at once.

"She will live," Harry told him. But Paul knew what Harry's words were saying without the need for any other words.

Chapter 19

The sunny day of promise that had begun this morning in Czestochowa had become a gray, blustery evening that threatened rain.

By the time Paul reached the center of the city. the wind had also picked up. Above, at the top of the slow rise of land where Jasna Gora sat, Paul saw nothing but a steel grayness of sky that hung above the monastery. Any patches of blue that had tried to shine through earlier were chastened now by sullen and gusty clouds.

Paul was fortunate enough to find a parking spot near the hospital so that he could quickly run inside the small, three-storied building wedged between row houses and office buildings. This was a hospital that saw little use, although that was sure to change when the Nazis invaded. Czestochowa was small, and except for heat exhaustion cases among the pilgrims to Jasna Gora and the birthings and dyings of local residents, the hospital was usually underutilized.

Once inside, Paul made an attempt at looking presentable by running his fingers through his unruly hair and by straightening a very crooked tie. A hospital orderly in the hall saw his distraction and immediately pointed to the Medical Director's office at the end of the first floor.

"She came through surgery satisfactorily," a short little man in a white medical coat said in answer to Paul's request for information about Sandra. "Her vital signs are good. We have managed to stop the bleeding and stitch the cuts. There was one piece of luck. Another half inch and the knife would have cut the eye," said Dr. Konrad Milander, whose name Paul noted from the name tag on his coat.

A piece of good luck. Paul repeated the phrase to himself. What luck could there be when a face had been cut from ear to ear, as Sandra's had been?

"Thank God for that," Paul said in response to the doctor's words.

"She will need plastic surgery and physical therapy, neither of which are specialties here at this hospital," Dr. Milander warned. "But that won't be needed until later."

Later, Paul thought. *And for what good?*

A door opened down the hall and de Wiart came out of Sandra's room on hearing Paul speaking to Dr. Milander. De Wiart's exhaustion was apparent.

De Wiart looked at Dr. Milander. "Can you give us a private room to talk to each other?"

"Of course."

De Wiart spoke first when they were alone. "Thank you, Paul, for all that you have done. As for Sandra, she saved my life."

That she did. But she didn't follow my directions. That's why she got hurt. Paul could never fault her for loving de Wiart so much that she went after Walter herself. However, Paul believed that de Wiart hadn't sent her the additional guards Paul had asked for. That was the truth that Paul wanted to shout to the world. But he knew the world would not believe him. It was his instinct for self preservation that warned him not to bring up the topic. He had no proof, and even if he did, Paul was aware that he would lose the battle.

De Wiart looked away for a minute. "Her condition has been stabilized--" he began, his voice trailing away. "But she needs specialized care that she can't get here. According to Dr Milander, her recuperation will be lengthy. And there's something else to consider."

Paul waited for the other man to speak.

"The Nazis will be here in three days. When that happens, the situation will be chaotic. There will be an enormous scarcity of medical help throughout all of Poland."

"In other words, we should get Sandra out of Poland today,'" said Paul. "How about Sandra's condition, Dr. Milander? Can she travel today?"

The doctor nodded. "We can give her fresh dressings for her wounds and make her comfortable with some sedatives for the flight back."

"Then let's do it," said Paul.

"There's just one problem," said de Wiart. "Sandra doesn't want to leave me. But I must stay here. You understand that. I will never break my promise. And what about her? She needs a higher level of medical care than can be provided here in war time."

"Let me speak to her," said Paul.

♦

The window shades were closed and her room was dark.

Paul looked at the completely swathed face of the fragile woman in the bed. Unable to talk, she was probably medicated to relieve her pain, Paul surmised.

When he took her hand in his, she squeezed it. He squeezed in return, bending over her so that she would hear his words without having to move. His voice was soft and tender as he spoke to her. "It's PS, GG. You are one of the bravest persons I know. You saved de Wiart's life all by yourself. But now you have to be even more courageous, my dear. You must let de

Wiart know that he has your blessing to stay here in Poland and help the Poles to fight the Nazis."

He felt her attempt to take her hand from his, but he held it even tighter.

Paul knew the words that would convince her. "But he won't be able to do his job if he is worrying that you are not getting the medical care that you need here in Poland. You must be braver than you have ever been. Let him stay here with your blessing. The Poles need him. Tell us that you agree to let us take you back to London."

Her hand was still. He took that for a "yes." Paul kissed her hand. "I'll leave you now with Dr. Milander and de Wiart. I will be back shortly to take you home. We love you, Sandra."

Then he looked at de Wiart. "I would like permission from you for us to take Lech and Maria Stepic back to London with us. They have skills we need to fight this war. Besides, the Nazis will soon know about what they did today. It wouldn't be too wise to allow them to stay here."

"And there is something else for us to discuss now. Can we talk about it outside this room for a minute?" de Wiart asked.

He asked for Paul's help in settling the Walter Schellenberg affair. He explained what his ideas were about how to do this.

"Do what you think needs to be done," said Paul. He left the decision to de Wiart. He would be the one leading a horrendous battle in the future.

De Wiart thanked him and left the room.

After that, Paul met with Harry and Dave. They should coordinate their flight plans with de Wiart. "The sooner the better," Paul emphasized.

"There's something else to consider," Harry said. "We found these papers in Schellenberg's pockets and in his suitcase." Harry held out a filled bag. "Dave and I think you should read all this as soon as possible," he said.

"I'll read it on the flight," said Paul.

As their plane climbed into the sky and headed for England, Paul watched the tall, fragile figure of de Wiart on the runway as he waved goodby to them. Paul quickly corrected himself. It wasn't goodby that de Wiart was saying. Instead he was promising them that one day they would all be able to return to Poland. Paul knew that de Wiart's overriding desire was to save Poland. Paul was also aware that in order to do that de Wiart would stop at nothing. The thought frightened Paul.

Soon the plane was flying too high for de Wiart to be seen.

Chapter 20

"Controlled disorder" was the term which Paul used to describe to Harry and David the work flow that began the day after they returned to Alnwyk.

As for Alnwyk, they learned when they returned that Bill had donated the castle to the country as the central location from which Paul would operate his branch of intelligence.

"It's a good choice," conceded Harry when he heard about it. "The estate is isolated and the fact that it can be easily guarded is a real plus."

Paul nodded. Although he was disappointed that he would not be operating out of Switzerland as Bill Stephenson had once promised him, he understood the advantages of using Alnwyk as headquarters for their Special Intelligence headquarters.

"As for Bill Stephenson, I can't keep up with him," Paul complained.

Although it was only a day since their return from Poland, Paul was already physically worn. More and more Bill turned to him for decisions. Privately, Paul wondered whether twenty four hours a day would be sufficient to meet the inordinate demands Stephenson was placing on him. "Can you do this?" or "Will you stop that project you are working on and begin this?" were questions Paul was learning to dread. However, in Bill's defense, and as Paul certainly understood, building a new intelligence system from scratch was no easy project. As for Stephenson, Paul wondered how much Bill knew about de

Wiart's connection with Sandra. However, it didn't matter, he told himself, for it really seemed true that each day at Alnwyk would probably begin and end with the Enigma /Ultra project which Paul would plan and staff, using the materials the Poles had given them. Luckily Paul would be able to delegate tasks to Harry and David, and others equally talented, like Maria and Lech Stepic, knowing that they would be done properly.

Then there was the matter of Walter Schellenberg's papers, the papers that David and Harry had given him on leaving Poland. As he had promised, Paul read everything on the trip back to London.

What he read was so explosive that Paul immediately made plans to cancel some important meetings he had scheduled for the afternoon in order to meet with Harry and David. Wanting privacy the three of them had gone outdoors to sit around a table in a rather isolated back patio of the estate.

"What do you make of this?" Paul picked up a sheet. "This is an official German interoffice memo to Walter which confirms that Walter had Hans Oster, Admiral Canaris' second in command, followed after the von Ribbentrop reception in London. During the surveillance Oster met with de Wiart for approximately thirty five minutes at an apartment in Kensington. The author of the memo has no information to offer as to what the conversation was about."

Paul picked up another sheet from Walter's papers. He held it up, saying, "What about this?'

"It's probably the most explosive information of all," said Dave. "It's anonymous, which makes it even more dangerous. It is a copy of a note sent to *Reichsfuhrer* Heinrich Himmler, Walter's boss, supposedly from a Polish Nazi sympathizer. Himmler sent Walter a copy of the letter and ordered him to return to Berlin as soon as possible. In the letter Walter is accused of having been turned by Sandra Martin into a source for the British. Walter's mother is also accused by the writer of being a Jew. The original letter to Himmler supposedly included a birth certificate to prove the charge that was made."

"And there is more?" said Paul.

"Plenty more," Harry said. "We wondered at first if the memo and the letter might be fakes. So this morning we checked with the informer we have in German Intelligence. Walter did receive a report about a meeting between Oster and de Wiart. He kept it secret, though, probably hoping that ultimately he would take credit for everything after he destroyed Canaris and Oster."

"Best of all, we were able to trace the typewriter that the anonymous letter was written on. That wasn't a difficult task because we already had several samples of letters typed on that machine. The typewriter has a very distinctive type face," said Harry.

"And?" Paul was almost screaming in impatience at this point.

"De Wiart sent that letter to Himmler. Or more precisely he probably dictated it for someone on his staff to type."

Paul put this sheet down and picked up another memo. "Let's look at everything first and then we'll analyze this bit by bit. This last piece is a memo from you two"—he looked at Harry and David intently--"which discusses information you received from Maria Stepic about her conversation at the Jasna Gora Monastery with Sandra Martin. Is that right?" They nodded.

David tried to explain. "Maria said that Sandra's speech sounded garbled and confused that afternoon, as if she were on drugs. Nothing she said seemed connected, such as describing herself as De Wiart 's special assistant or saying that she was on assignment from de Wiart to destroy Walter in any way that she could. She also told Maria that she took her directions directly from de Wiart and not from you, Paul. She wasn't to fear Walter. She said that de Wiart's men would always protect her.

"We questioned Maria thoroughly. We're certain what she says was the truth. I don't think she left anything out or exaggerated about anything," explained Harry.

"Nor do I," said Paul. "I see no reason to doubt her comments about Sandra. Did Maria say why she told you all this?"

"Maria thought you needed to know this in light of what happened to Sandra at the Monastery. Maria also said that she had heard you warn Sandra not to antagonize Walter and provoke him. And yet that was exactly what she did. Her behavior might have been caused by drugs. Her eyes seemed glassy and her speech was slurred," said Harry.

"I did a little checking about that," admitted David. "When I had a few minutes to myself when we were on the plane I searched through Sandra's handbag. Here is what I found." He held up two bottles containing very strong tranquilizers. On both labels de Wiart was listed as the patient.

Paul felt drained. "Give me a minute or two to digest all this, will you?"

The three of them were quiet for a while, thinking about what they had just learned.

David spoke first. "None of it makes sense until you put it in a logical order."

"So?" asked Harry impatiently.

"Hold your horses and let me explain. It all starts with the rivalry between Canaris and Himmler. From what I've heard, Himmler and his top henchman, Walter, were well on their way to proving Canaris' involvement in a plot to persuade top German military leaders to get rid of Hitler and thus prevent war. To do this Canaris needed to get the support of the world against Hitler, discredit Himmler, and hopefully eliminate

Schellenberg. And how best to achieve those goals?" David waited for an answer.

"Of course," said Harry. "A good way would be to get a leading icon like de Wiart to be on your side. De Wiart would not only be working for peace, but he would be convincing the Poles to stand up to the Nazis as well. If war is inevitable, as many think, perhaps the best Carnaris can do at this point is to allow others like de Wiart to turn everyone against the Nazis."

Paul nodded. "But what about Sandra? Does she have a part in this or not?" He thought for a minute. "Of course she does. How could I be so stupid?"

"You aren't stupid. But explain," said David.

"De Wiart will always be a Polish hero, and rightfully so. But don't you see what he is doing? By encouraging Sandra to enrage Walter enough so that he might attack her, she becomes a heroine, someone everyone will use to rally around and fight for. De Wiart deliberately countermanded my directions to her in order to put her in harm's way. In other words, he made her live bait. And from what you are telling me he deliberately brainwashed and drugged Sandra so that she would willingly play the part he gave her. She would be a way to get rid of Walter. She might kill him or he might kill her. It didn't matter. Either dead or alive, Sandra would wind up a heroine to inspire the world about the rightness of fighting the Nazis."

"But that was cruel," said Paul.

"Perhaps one has to be cruel in order to be an icon," said Harry.

David found that hard to buy. And he had another question. "But how do the pieces fit together, Paul? Was everything about our trip to Poland one big hoax? Were we really there to cover up the fact that something other than plans for jet propulsion was being taken out of Poland?"

“We certainly were,” Paul said. ”That was true. But what de Wiart also realized was that he could get lots of sympathy and possibly additional public support if he brought Sandra into the story. It seems to me that he didn’t care whether she lived or died as long as her bravery resulted in lots of public sympathy for the Polish cause.”

But Paul knew that he owed Harry and David an explanation. “I have never given you the specific facts about what was leaving Poland before the Nazis could get their hands on it. In fact, I can’t give you any more of an explanation right now for fear of compromising what is an important state secret. But when I can, you two will be the first to know.”

“And then there’s the bottom line,” Harry said. “What happens now to de Wiart? He shouldn’t get away with what he did.”

Paul had made his decision and he would follow it. ”No, he shouldn’t but yes, he will,” he said.

Harry and David weren’t satisfied with that.

“We do nothing about de Wiart,” emphasized Paul. “Icons make their own rules, especially in wartime. The fact that de Wiart has been several steps ahead of us in planning for the war he will be fighting doesn’t mean that he has done anything illegal. All it means is that we have been slow to understand what was happening. Will I ever forget his cruelty to Sandra? I promise you that one day I will make him regret it. But right now Poland desperately needs de Wiart’s help.”

“Point taken,” said Harry. He didn’t want to agree, but he did understand Paul’s reason. “But what about a Review Board evaluation?” he asked. Every intelligence activity in the British CIS received an evaluation review when the operation was over. Usually the review was just a matter of form, although Paul had seen the careers of others made or destroyed by the whims of those on review boards.

"I haven't heard anything about a review board for our Polish trip," said Paul.

Then that was that. Their assignment in Poland was over. For the most part, it had turned out successfully.

Now it was time to move on and face what everyone knew was fast approaching.

That arrived very shortly.

In fact, the Nazi *blitzkrieg* against Poland came on the exact day that de Wiart had said it would. The news from Poland was dire indeed. From the patchy communication which existed, the world learned with horror of the almost complete devastation that had struck Poland. Warsaw as well as other cities were said to have almost disappeared. The Polish government was forced to leave the country. Although Polish soldiers fought the Nazis, the fact that the rest of the world reneged on its promises to help Poland meant that Poland possessed no adequate resources to fight for its life.

As for de Wiart, he proved too wily for the Nazis to catch. Although he continued to lead some troops in sections of Poland that were still fighting, resistance to the Nazis became impossible since the Poles had little left to fight with. However, de Wiart was lying in wait for the time when the tide would turn, although even he admitted that would be long in coming.

To the group at Alnwyk Sandra became a huge worry for everyone. In fact, the best that could be said about her condition as well as her attitude was that both were problematic. It was clear that the optimistic view which Sandra first held about her injuries was not realistic. At first she had done a good job of handling the high level of pain her wounds caused. However, when the London surgeons attempted to give her a realistic assessment of what they could accomplish, she refused to listen, slipping into a depression that no one was able to penetrate. By now she had quietly retreated into her own world. Her friends accepted her behavior as normal, given the awfulness of her wounds. Although these improved somewhat from the plastic surgery she received, Sandra knew that they would never be gone. This was what she was unable to accept.

Surprisingly, the one person she would talk to was Paul. Even Bill and his wife, once her best friends, were now excluded from her rooms. Sandra was hurt when old friends of hers like Friedrich-Werner von der Schulenburg never bothered to even call or come to see her. But Paul was different. She believed that he cared about her. Because she seemed to look forward to seeing him, Paul was optimistic that their conversations might ultimately pull her back into the world. At least he would try.

However, as time went on, Paul realized that what Sandra wanted from him was a friendly ear that would listen as she talked about her past, someone who would encourage her almost disjointed ramblings about the past by smiling at the right points or by nodding when an answer was appropriate.

She actually laughed when he used the nicknames she had chosen for them.

Increasingly their conversations centered on her father. She had obviously adored the man, although more and more Paul wondered about the healthiness of that love. Had it been Max who was responsible for her inability to relate to the world in appropriate ways?

One day Paul decided to shock Sandra into understanding the extent of Max's lopsided importance in her life. In the middle of one of her long accounts about a trip she and Max had taken, Paul threw out a question designed to startle her. "Max was a daughter fucker, wasn't he, Sandra?" He deliberately stared into her lovely eyes as he said the words.

"Wasn't he, Sandra?" He repeated his question quietly when she didn't respond.

The lovely lilac eyes turned to ice. "That may be true, but it's far from being the entire story."

He persisted. "And what is that?"

"I was no victim, nor will I ever be a victim, even if you try to make me into one. As for Max being a daughter fucker, the truth is that I was a father fucker first."

He started to speak, but she cut him off with a flick of her fingers in a "go away" motion. Although he pleaded with her to talk to him she turned her head and never again spoke to him. No one other than the medical staff could ever enter her rooms again.

After that, days turned into a week before Paul received a telephone call from de Wiart's headquarters. De Wart himself would be coming to England tomorrow to be with Sandra, Paul was told. There was also a message from de Wiart for him, the voice went on. Would Paul see to it that no one knew that he was coming? De Wiart wanted no one else there. Was that possible, the voice asked.

"Of course," said Paul. The time was set for de Wiart's arrival.

♦

Only Paul was standing outside the front of Alnwyk when the limousine pulled up and a chauffeur jumped out to open a door for de Wiart.

The two men greeted each other and spoke for a few minutes before they went into the house and sat down in the drawing room.

"I brought you something," de Wiart said. He went to the door and clicked his fingers at the waiting butler, explaining what the man was to get from de Wiart's car.

"I thought that this would be a reminder of how you helped Poland on that day at Jasna Gora Monastery." Paul ripped off the paper surrounding the package De Wiart gave him.

"It's a print of the Holy Virgin, known in Czestochowa as the Black Madonnna. Those eyes are haunting with their sadness," said de Wiart. "I want you to have it for saving my life that day."

Paul nodded. "Thank you. And thank Sandra. She saved your life. I only wish that we could have prevented her injuries." Paul wanted to ask de Wiart what had happened to the extra guards supposedly assigned to Sandra. But he didn't. He had no proof. None at all. There was no way of winning this one.

"I, too," whispered de Wiart. "But like the pilgrims whose faith leads them to the Monastery and the Madonna, I have faith that God has a plan for our lives, although we may not always see it."

It was all Paul could do to contain his desire to lash out at de Wiart. *"God's will,"* Paul repeated to himself. *Let's rephrase that to "De Wiart's will." That's all de Wiart believes in.*

De Wiart walked back to a chair and sat. "How is she?" he asked.

Paul had to be honest. "Sandra's depression is serious," he said. There was nothing more that medicine could do, according to the doctors.

De Wiart nodded. "Then I will take her back to Poland with me. It might remove her depression if she helps people who are in worse shape that she is."

"I think you may be right, sir. Staying here any longer is not helping her."

"Then let's do it now. Take me to her room and then alert the maid that she is to pack Sandra's suitcases immediately. We'll leave as soon as possible. However, I hope that before I leave we can talk."

Paul realized that he wanted one last word with Sandra. "Stay," he implored her. "We'll help you find yourself."

She looked at him for a long while before she entered the limousine. "I have no desire to be found," she said with no emotion in her voice.

Without any more fanfare or any last goodbye, Sandra left Alnwyk for the last time with de Wiart at her side.

As they left, Paul looked at de Wiart, thinking of the secret that they shared. Both were aware Sandra had been de Wiart's victim, irrespective of how one chooses to describe his use of her. He had deliberately sacrificed her to Walter's fury, obviously believing that whether she died or lived was immaterial. What was material to de Wiart was that she be an icon for the people to follow. And yet in spite of knowing that he was talking and smiling back at de Wiart as if the man had not done anything that warranted censure, Paul continued to smile. *My smile is not the truth,* he thought, *but it is what de Wiart expects and what I am obligated to give him.* Suddenly Paul wanted to have done with all falseness. He promised himself that he would never again believe that a lie or an exaggeration could be made into the truth. Truth was truth. At the very least he hoped that his life would always be a testament to knowing what the truth was, even if he could not always speak it.

That day was the last time he would ever see Sandra.

The pain he saw in her face as she looked at him from the back window of the limousine seemed to Paul to reflect the same perception of life that the Black Madonna painting portrayed. For each, life had been a journey which traveled from knowledge to understanding in order to find life's ultimate meaning, Like the unhappiness on the Black Madonna's face, Sandra's travels had also revealed to her that sadness resides at the core of life. As for de Wiart, Paul was never certain whether that man who sat beside Sandra in the long black limousine as it took her away was her savior or her executioner. But did it matter to de Wiart? Paul was reasonably certain that it didn't.

♦

Something utterly unexpected happened the following day after Sandra's departure.

"Stop what you are doing and look at this." Bill Stephenson raced down the hall to Paul's office, collecting curious people who wanted to know what all the noise was about.

"Look what's on the front page of many papers around the world, thanks to news services." Bill spread the first page of the *London Times* across Paul's conference table.

"Listen to this," said Bill.

Early risers in Berlin saw a different sight than usual when they passed by the Brandenburg Gate.

Today the dead body of Brigadefuhrer Walter Schellenberg was found hanging from a makeshift gallows that had been attached to the Gate.

Government officials described Schellenberg as one of the most important leaders within German intelligence. It is not yet known how Schellenberg died, although an autopsy today will be done to determine the cause of death.

Unidentified sources say that a signed note was found attached to the body. Although German government sources deny that any such note existed, the London Times has received a copy of what is purported to be in that note.

After that, the newspaper printed a copy of the note they said was found with the body.

<u>To All Germans</u>

We, the citizens of Poland, a country which you recently unjustly invaded and destroyed and in the process murdered many innocent people, are returning the body of Walter Schellenberg to you. His cruel acts and cowardice, as well as those of other Nazis who have turned Germany into a nation of murderers, have led to the invasion and destruction of not only Poland, but other countries as well.

Germany deserves condemnation from the world for its shameful actions.

(signed) **The Citizens of Poland**

The article ended with a photo that Paul, Harry, and David clearly identified as Sandra. Under the photo was the explanatory paragraph below.

Attached is a photo of a woman identified only as Sasha who is said to have killed Schellenberg in order to keep him from murdering British Lieutenant General Androz de Wiart, a man described by Polish government leader Nladyslaw Sikorski as a hero fighting for Poland's right to exist.

Paul looked up after he finished reading the material. "That should be helpful in marshalling public support for getting into the war against Germany," he said.

"You were right, Paul," said Harry. "De Wiart will use Sandra to get as much support as he can."

Paul nodded. "De Wiart has the ability to mold public opinion. But then we can always ask whether war is sufficient justification for saying a wrong was right. Does war make a wrong right? Probably not, but in a time of war what *is* right, anyhow? Stay for a few minutes, will you?" Paul said to Harry and Paul when others were drifting back to their offices. There are a few things that the three of us have to decide before tomorrow."

Harry smiled. "You have just answered your own question, Paul."

"How so?"

"Perhaps wartime does give humanity a way of assuaging its conscience about right and wrong, for like time, it just marches on to the next problem that needs to be solved. Just as we are doing," said Harry.

Harry had been right to question Paul about whether there would be a Review Board session.

Only a day went by after Sandra left before Paul got a call from Bill Stephenson. "Stop by my office about two this afternoon, will you, Paul?" Bill's voice sounded unusual, with a slight edge of excitement as well as an obvious effort to contain any emotion in his voice. "We need to get a review board session out of the way for the Polish trip. Standard procedure, you know," Bill said, obviously attempting to make his a casual request.

"Of course," said Paul, equally casual. When he hung up, he turned a puzzled face to Harry and Dave and relayed Bill's words. None of them could figure out what this meant, but no one seemed unduly upset, except for Paul, who wanted this over and done with. After all, it was his career at stake, wasn't it?

Promptly at two, Paul knocked on the massive hand-carved door that led to Bill's suite of offices.

A secretary then smilingly led him through a portrait gallery that the staff had jokingly decided to call "The For God and Country Portrait Corridor." Every English monarch and what seemed to be every Alnwyk ancestor had his or her face emblazoned on that wall. Unsmiling twits, those ancestors, weren't they? thought Paul.

Undeterred by the elegance that surrounded her, Bill's secretary briskly knocked on the door before opening it herself and announcing Paul's name and rank to a filled room. Paul blinked, for there were at least fifteen people smiling at him, all cabinet level rank or Parliamentary leaders.

Bill was now at his elbow, skillfully leading Paul to the center of the library section of Bill's office. He turned to Paul, smiled, and waved his hand as a way to get everyone's attention.

"This is to illustrate our thanks, Paul, for your successful trip to Poland. We wish you well now that you are based here." Stephenson had already told Paul that his new title was Director of Staff Communications, but as he and only a few others knew, it meant that he would be directing the super secret Ultra/Enigma Project, the outgrowth of the materials which the Poles had given to the English.

Bill looked at his watch. "Luncheon will be served in twenty minutes."

"Come sit with me," came the familiar voice of someone sitting on a large comfortable sofa facing a window. Winston Churchill patted the seat next to him. As he sat, Paul observed how the others surrounding Churchill discreetly moved so that he and Churchill might have a quiet moment together.

"We are pleased with your performance, Paul. I couldn't be happier than I am at having you with us."

"Thank you, sir," said Paul, who felt uneasy at the recognition he was receiving. It wasn't that he was shy, but he was never at ease being in the public eye.

"Makes one feel like a prize bull being exhibited, doesn't it?" asked Churchill, who had shrewdly observed Paul's unease at this recognition.

"It's all right, sir," Paul said. "Just as long as I'm not a heifer being carted off to the slaughter house."

Churchill laughed at that. "Sit beside me at lunch today. We'll get pleasantly drunk together. We deserve it."

Paul's smile lit up his face. "It would be an honor and a pleasure, sir. I'll hold you to that offer."

"Oh, incidentally, the Review Board report is on Bill's desk. A copy of it is there for your records. We asked de Wiart to write the report. He wrote a glowing review of your work. Congratulations." Churchill reached out his hand for Paul to help him from the sofa. "And now on to bigger and better pursuits in the dining room."

Before the afternoon had passed, Paul at one point saw that Bill Stephenson was looking intently at him. The look allowed Paul to believe that Bill knew what de Wiart had done.

So much for a Review Board's absence of questions about what happened to Sandra Martin on that day at Josna Gora.

♦

A few days after the Review Board session, Paul's secretary scurried around the building, intent on finding her boss. Paul had a habit of finding and burrowing in quieter places than his busy office when he wanted to think.

Jane finally found him in the library, one of his favorite hiding spots.

"You have a visitor," Jane informed him in a breathless and rather annoyed voice.

"Who is it?" he said without looking up.

"Here is her card. I've asked her to sit in the waiting room."

Paul looked at the name and instantly bolted up from his chair to run down the hall to the waiting room. When he got there he stood outside the door and gazed through the glass panels so that his eyes might stare for a while without having to say a word. He experienced a happiness so intense that his entire body tingled. Again and again he yelled a name, *her* name.

Alexa ran out of the room to join him. He held her tightly in his arms, still repeating her name again and again as if it were a magical incantation that would ultimately take one into another universe the more it was said.

She was crying now. "After you left Switzerland I realized that having you in my life is all that matters to me. Not Andrei, or hurting him, or anything else in the world. You are all that matters. I told Andrei that I didn't want to be his wife. He understands, and I believe that he accepts it." Alexa giggled. "To tell the truth, I believe he knows in his heart that he'll be happier by himself."

Paul nodded.

She touched his face. "I was afraid that you wouldn't want me. But I had to come to you. I had no choice."

"No, you didn't have a choice, and I'm glad of it."

"I want to divorce Andrei immediately and marry you. Will you have me?"

"Look at my face for your answer, darling. And ask Mariana if she wants to stay in Switzerland during the war or would she rather live here with us," he said.

Alexa said that she would ask her.

After that, they returned to practicalities by choosing dates and times for her divorce and their marriage. Would she mind living here in the Alnwyk grounds? There were many nice cottages, he told her. She liked that. "We will survive the Nazis," he told her confidently.

He looked at her glowing and radiant face as they made plans for their future. Hers, like Sandra's, was also the face of a madonna. Although the Black Madonna's eyes stress life's pain and suffering, the joyous child that the Madonna held in her arms reminded Paul of Alexa, for whom life would also be a search for happiness as well as an understanding that pain and suffering may also be part of that quest.

Everything, allowed Paul, might be a reflection of God's will, as De Wiart had said. However, even if true, it is still necessary to rely on one's self in order to know the parameters of the happiness that life can provide. But such a reality exists, whether it inheres in the beauty of a smile or in the passage of a breathtaking life. Paul was certain that everything was findable, but only when one understood what one was searching for.

Chapter 21

Epilogue

After the Nazi Invasion of Poland

"Bill Stephenson has just given me the go ahead to explain to you why our trip to Poland took place," Paul told Harry and Dave not long after that memorable Review Board meeting.

"At last," Harry said, although Paul was uncertain about whether he said it enthusiastically or sarcastically.

However, after Paul completed his explanation, both men immediately apologized to Paul if he thought that they had at any time attempted to pressure him into giving them an explanation.

Paul said, "No. I understand your desire to know. But believe me, wild horses couldn't have dragged the truth from me any earlier, no matter how much you tried."

The truth was simple. And yet in its simplicity lay the subtlety of its power. The story that they spread about wanting to find Jan Babij's jet propulsion plans in Krakow was just that: a story, but a diversionary story, at best. The real story concerned what was happening at the same time in a section of Poland very far from the Krakow area where they were.

"Our excuse that we were in Krakow attempting to find Jan Babij's plans for making jet propulsion planes? That was pure hookum," added Paul.

So? Why then had they been there? "The real reason was extraordinary," said Paul, as he began to explain. Because a Nazi attack on Poland was imminent in 1939, Poland made a startling offer to England. Poland was going to give England a working model of the first deciphering electromechanical computer ever produced in the world, a Polish creation complete with specifications, perforated cards and updating procedures for reading "Enigma," the major German military code.

The significance of Poland's gift to England of this deciphering computer is almost incalculable.

As Winston Churchill later said after the war, the fact that the British had this capability hastened the ending of World War II by at least two years.

"By using a computer developed by linguists, mathematicians, and engineers in Poland, the Polish intelligence services broke the German "Enigma" code earlier in 1932-1933," explained Paul to his staff. "We are in the process now of incorporating this into a high-speed deciphering program we call Ultra."

"If the Germans ever discover that the British have this capability, they will immediately change the German codes, making the system obsolete." Paul pointed out.

"Security for the project will be enormous," Paul said to Harry and Dave when he appointed them and explained their responsibilities. "The two of you will help me set up and run Ultra," Paul said to the surprised men. That was the name given to the project.

♦

The years that followed were times of high stress given over to high security war time activities for the three men as well as the additional Cold War stresses which followed the end of World War II.

For the entire time, Paul and his assistants, Harry and David, so skillfully directed the program that the Germans never learned, or even suspected, that their codes were being broken so successfully.

As for the importance of the project, all the papers relating to it were sealed for a fifty-year period after the war.

Finally, with the war over and the Communist presence eliminated from Poland, Paul and his two assistants had an itch to once again see the Poland that they remembered so vividly from their 1939 trip. Alexa also wanted to join the three men on this second trip to Poland. Her desire to go might be a good idea, Paul decided. It might make what was certain to be an emotional visit easier for him to bear.

Before they left England for their second trip to Poland, they hardened themselves to some obvious facts.

As Dave noted, after all these years the Poles they remembered and the sites where they had stayed in Poland were probably gone. Wouldn't that fact alone make the trip a depressing one?

"But so what?" Paul countered. "In 1939 we made a promise that one day we would return to Poland," Paul said. "The trip will be a positive recognition by us that Poland won its battle to exist."

That settled it. The trip was on.

Instead of a tour of the entire country, though, the group decided to visit only the same places that they had seen on the first trip. Alexa, the one who had never been to Poland, liked the itinerary they established. "But be prepared," she warned them. "Thomas Wolfe says that no one can never go home again."

"But he's wrong," insisted Paul. "We aren't going back expecting to see the same Poland. All we want to celebrate is that Poland had the will and strength to save itself."

"Paul's right." said Harry. "That's all we want."

"Then let's go to Krakow," said Paul.

♦

When their plane arrived. Paul stared at the still war-torn Polish countryside. Krakow had not been as damaged by the Nazis as the other cities in Poland for one reason only. The Nazis had chosen the city as the capital city for the Nazi wartime government in Poland. However, the war and its Communist aftermath had not been kind at all to any of the Poles.

Memories flooded Paul's mind as soon as they arrived in Krakow. The first one that crossed his mind was that in 1939 an aura of uncertainty had seemed to hover over the country. No one knew what to expect. Would Poland be attacked or was the fear of war unwarranted?

But now, years later, instead of uncertainty, a sense of exhaustion appeared to cover the country. And rightly so, thought Paul as he remembered the tragedy that Poland had become. Over seven million people had died or been murdered in Poland since 1939, Paul thought. The number was so huge so he could not begin to comprehend its enormity. Where were those in 1939 who should have been eliminating the need for war?

There certainly hadn't been many of those as leaders in 1939.

"Remember how we hated the appeasers in London who thought at the time that Hitler would never attack if the world met what he called his reasonable demands?" Paul asked.

"You are talking about those like Ambassador Kennedy who were willing to make any compromise or admit that white was black and black was white if it would convince Hitler not to attack?" Harry asked contemptuously.

"Yes. Them." said Paul. "Of course at the beginning of the war and even before it started there were some brave enough to try to unite the world by eliminating Hitler."

"Like Wilhelm Canaris, the senior intelligence officer in Germany who headed up the *Abwehr* military intelligence unit? By 1939 and even during the war he tried, but he wasn't successful at all in organizing a coup or even at attempting to be a peacemaker. Nor was anyone ever successful in changing Hitler's crazy ideas," Harry said.

"Far from being successful, Canaris was accused late in the war by Heinrich Himmler of being disloyal to Hitler," said Paul. "After a phony trial, Canaris and his assistant, Hans Oster, were hanged from the gallows and their bodies left on the gallows to rot."

There was a short silence after that. Harry said, "We met another casualty like Canaris in London back in 1939, didn't we?"

"You mean Friedrich-Werner von der Schulenburg, don't you?" asked Paul. "Sandra's friend."

Dave nodded. "Schulenburg had been a top German diplomat since 1903. But that didn't matter when Hitler made up his mind that Schulenburg was involved in an attempt on his life. He had him hanged late in the war."

"So much for those who got on the wrong side of Hitler, whether German or not," said Harry.

"And then of course, in 1939 as also today, there is a most important figure who weaves in and out of Polish activities at will," said Paul.

"Of course. That is Lieutenant-General Androz de Wiart," said Dave, enunciating each part of the name. It was obvious that de Wiart was not one of his favorite people. "Have you heard anything about de Wiart recently? He seems to have dropped out of the story in Poland very quickly. And what about Sandra? What have we heard about her?"

Paul shook his head. "I've heard very little about de Wiart since the end of the war and even less about Sandra. When the war began in 1939 de Wiart was appointed to his old job as head of the British Military Mission to Poland to help the Poles fight the Germans. However, when Polish resistance weakened, de Wiart was forced to evacuate his mission. After fighting in Romania, Norway, and Ireland, de Wiart served a brief time as an Italian prisoner of war. He was soon released and made his way to England. After a short time he was appointed as Churchill's special representative to China, a position he still holds," added Paul.

"But what about Sandra?" Harry persisted. "During the war years many press releases passed our desk about 'Sasha' and her activities in the Polish resistance during the war, but we never knew how much credence to give to them, although the stories inspired many Poles to fight the Nazis," he said.

"Nor do I," said Paul. "So I suggest that we accept what we have read and then move on." Privately Paul was afraid that he would never get rid of his guilt about Sandra. Had he done all he could to help her? He doubted that. *I would like to see her once more to tell her how sorry I am for what happened to her.*

Their trip began.

They structured their days so that there was no schedule that they had to rigidly adhere to.

In fact, they could eliminate a scheduled stop if they wished and go off on their own. "What would you like to visit once more?" asked Paul.

The Monastery of Jasna Gora in Czestochowa was everyone's first choice.

"I would like to relive the day we were there as much as I can," said Dave. He looked embarrassed, but not so much as to not share his thoughts with his friends. "I have to tell you that it was a day of emotion for me. Seeing the Black Madonna and understanding her message of hope affected me deeply. It was also a day of terrible evil. I like to think, though, that the Black Virgin won the day, just as she did the war."

For some reason the Germans had spared the Monastery during the war, although most of the small surrounding village of Czestochowa suffered relentless bombing. Although the Poles were not permitted to enter the Monastery during the war, the Germans allowed the Poles to clean and maintain the buildings properly during the German occupation.

They took one last look at the Monastery before they left. *Thank you,* Paul said wordlessly. The faith exemplified by Jasna Gora had helped pull the Poles through World War II.

They stopped off at Bielany to visit the Janusek chalet where they had stayed their first night in Poland in 1939. Once again they admired the lovely scenery on the way. On this trip they were able to take their time driving through the scenic Wolski Forest. When they came to the magnificent Church and Hermitage of the Camadolese Monks they knew that they must be approaching the little village of Bielany.

"The old beautiful Poland is still here," Dave said, relief obvious in his voice. "It just needs some dusting after being exposed to the dirt of the Nazi and Communist worlds." When they arrived at the village they were surprised to find it full of boys, ranging from toddlers to teenagers.

Dave got out of the car to speak to an older man who was talking to some of the boys. When he returned to the car he told everyone that this was now a home for orphan boys. He had gotten the name and address of the administrator he spoke to. "We'll send the orphanage a nice check when we get back home," he said.

And now on to Ojcow.

With joy and high expectations they pulled up to the front door of the Wajda Guest house. In their minds each could visualize the short, sturdy body of Helga Wajda who had run to meet them in 1939 with joy in her eyes about the dinner she was preparing in their honor.

But now no one was there to greet them.

Paul sucked in his breath and shrugged his shoulders in sadness. He consoled himself by saying that the past times would always be preserved in his memory and he would never lose them. Never.

However, someone was now shuffling out of the main house.

"I am Rosa Majda," a woman said in a voice that obviously had grown accustomed to whispering. But the smile on her face said that she remembered them. "Helga was my mother," she said.

They all picked up on that past tense reference.

"My mother, my father, all my sisters, and my husband were bayoneted by the Nazis who caught them when we fought at the beginning of the war in Warsaw. I escaped with my infant son." She pushed strands of hair from her eyes. "I live here with my son now. And his wife and daughter."

A gaunt woman and a man old beyond his years walked hesitantly out of the house behind Rosa. The woman held a toddler in her arms.

Rosa said, "We manage to grow enough to feed ourselves. Please be our guests tonight. We will be glad to share what we have with you."

"We would love to eat with you. However, only if you allow us to provide the food," offered Paul.

It had been Alexa's good idea to stop at a store in Krakow when they landed to buy canned food as well as packaged food that did not need any refrigeration. "We don't know when we'll need it," she had warned.

"We'll get the food out of our car trunk and bring it to your kitchen," Paul said to the family. "You wait here."

They tried not to look at the Wajda Guest House as they passed it on their way to the car to get the food. The cheerful brown cedar house was falling down. The roof shingles hung haphazardly, Tall weeds were everywhere. Paul cringed when he saw the ominous sign that had been nailed to what had once been the cheerful yellow front door of the Wajda home. "Land for sale," it announced. Obviously the house was doomed to be torn down.

Paul ran ahead of everyone for the last few steps to the car. He opened the door so that he could rest his head on the steering wheel. They heard the sounds of crying. His tears came freely.

His friends surrounded him silently, anxious to help but not knowing what to do. This was the first time during all the years that they had known him that they had ever seen Paul cry.

Eventually his tears slowed down. *They don't know why I am crying, and I can't tell them,* he thought. His were more than tears for a past that was gone. They were tears because he felt unable to sufficiently mourn for that past. There was much that he wanted to honor with tears. But he couldn't recapture the intensity of what had happened. The silence of the past was too overwhelming, and the anger, the fear, and, yes, the guilt he had once felt in the past had all fused into the immediacy of the presence. *My feelings deserve more than I can give them,* he thought brokenly. But wasn't that what life always did to the past? Wasn't it always relegated to a nothingness that humanity attempts to apologize for by erecting buildings or statues? *I am sorry, Sandra. You deserved more than I gave you.*

He turned to his friends when his tears stopped. "I know what I want to do," he said to them. Once again his eyes showed the fire of the old Paul. "I'm going to buy this property and turn it back into the guest house this once was," he announced.

"What a wonderful idea," Alexa said with excitement. "And you will keep Wanda's Well?"

Of course they would maintain the entire property as it once had been, promised David. Harry and Dave also agreed that they would teach Rosa how to run the place.

"And we'll all come here for our vacations," said Paul.

When Paul explained their plans, Rosa and her family were amazed and touched that anyone would want to help them. The group stayed for several more days in the Ojcow area than they had planned in order to finalize the sale and begin the restoration.

♦

Paul and the others were content with what they had accomplished when their plane took off for home. They would return to Poland in several weeks to get the project underway.

As for Paul, life had taught him no matter how pretty it is to believe that one can make the world a better place than it is, the idea is inherently unrealistic. But he believed that he had found a viable solution. By the time they restored the Wajda Guest House, the world would be able to boast that once again it possessed a brown cedar shake home with pink heart-shaped wooden window shutters and a shiny yellow front door. In his dreams he would always see a certain lovely woman with the most lilac of eyes happily entering the house in order to be with her friends.

That dream would bring him happiness.

29619094R00145

Made in the USA
San Bernardino, CA
29 January 2016